The Courtship of Camellia
by
Michele Shriver

SMC Publishing

Chapter One

Her clothes all but stuck to her body in the stifling humidity of early September, though she wore only a linen shirt in a delicate pink and white capri pants. Paired with sandals, it was a smart outfit and the pink of her toenails—she made sure she got a pedicure before leaving on the trip—matched the pink of her top. All in all, Camellia was pleased with her appearance. At her age, and with her physical challenges, she couldn't always say that. Still, she'd left home that morning feeling good about herself and about the weekend ahead of her.

And then she stepped off the plane in Miami.

Texas was hot in September, often unbearably so, but even its misery couldn't compare to Florida, and Camellia wondered why this conference couldn't be held in a milder climate. She didn't even like palm trees or flamingos, and it wasn't as if she planned on doing much swimming while she was there. No thanks. A bathing suit on her body would surely scare the locals.

"Remind me again why coming to Miami in September seemed like a good idea," Camellia muttered to herself as she stepped out of her rental car. The air conditioner had finally decided to kick in right before she got to the hotel, and now she was hit with another blast of humidity.

"I was thinking the same thing. I hate this city. Yet here I am."

The man's voice jolted Camellia from her own mini pity party, as she'd been trying to figure out how to get her luggage into the hotel.

She'd had help with her suitcase as she navigated her way from the airport to her rental car, but now, naturally, everyone appeared to be arriving at the hotel at the same time, meaning the bellhops were scarce and Camellia was largely on her own. She could navigate her forearm crutches fine. She was a pro with those. But with a suitcase? That was another matter.

That thought was forgotten, though, when she heard the man's voice, which was vaguely familiar, and then looked up into his blue eyes, which were very familiar. These blue eyes didn't belong to a hotel bellhop. No. She knew these eyes. Heck, she used to dream about these eyes. Her, along with three quarters of the female population of Westfield High. Those eyes had been the source of many a schoolgirl fantasy back in the day.

That was more than twenty-five years ago, but she'd be damned if the eyes weren't still beautiful.

"Eric?" She squinted into the sun. "Eric Grady?" Yes, it was him, all right. She'd last seen him two years ago, when he emceed their class reunion. Eric had arrived with a hot brunette on his arm, and probably left with her, too. Camellia, meanwhile, got drunk with a couple of girlfriends while they ate fast food tacos.

"Yeah. Do I know you?" He studied her face, and Camellia couldn't decide if he was trying to recognize her or searching for a non-offensive way to disguise the fact that he didn't. "Oh, wait... Did you go to Westfield High? In Texas? Class of '95?"

So, he sort of remembered her. Maybe? "Yes. I spent my last two years of high school at Westfield." They hadn't been great years, but whatever. "I sat behind you in Mr. Miller's AP English Lit class." And hoped you would notice me, but you never did.

"That's right. And you were at the class reunion a couple years ago." Eric smiled. "Your name is Camellia, right?"

He did remember. A little bit. "Yes. Camellia Harris," she said. "It's a small world, isn't it?"

"I'll say. What brings you here?"

"Work. I'm here for a conference. On flowers. How about you?"

"Oh, hey, yeah. You work at a flower shop, right?" he asked. "Near Dallas?"

"Yes," she said. "I don't just work there, though. I own it."

"Wow. Good for you," Eric said. "I'm here for the flower show, too."

"You are?" Camellia blinked. "I wasn't aware you were in the business."

"Oh, I'm not. Not the flower business, anyway," he said. "I'll be your emcee. Master of Ceremonies." He smiled again, revealing perfect teeth. Some would say he was a little too pretty. He probably had been twenty-seven years ago, too, but Camellia liked pretty. At least from a distance, because pretty often meant asshole.

"That's what I do these days," Eric continued. "I travel around the country lending my face and my voice to corporate events and getting paid ridiculous amount of money for it."

"Sounds like fun." And it explained, sort of, why he'd hosted their class reunion. And here she thought it was only because he'd been Mr. Popularity back then.

Camellia reached back into the car to retrieve her crutches, wishing she could leave them behind. But tripping and falling as she walked into the hotel would embarrass her more than the crutches would, and sometimes it was a choice she had to make. Like right now.

She popped the trunk release of the car and placed her forearms into her braces to steady herself as she walked to the trunk, but she was still left with the same dilemma she had been a few minutes before.

"Do you need help with your luggage?" Eric asked.

She wanted to say no, insist she could do it herself, but that was ridiculous. "Yes, if you don't mind."

"Not at all." Eric reached into the trunk and lifted her suitcase out with ease. "I'm happy to carry it in for you. I got here a little bit ago, and things are a little backed up."

"Probably too many people arriving at once. It's a big conference." Camellia followed Eric into the hotel lobby, grateful for the blast of air-conditioning that greeted her. She would definitely not be spending much time outside while in Florida.

She approached the front desk to check in to her room, but when she asked for assistance with her luggage, though, Eric stepped forward. "I'll take it up to your room for you."

Camellia wasn't in the mood to argue, so she simply shrugged. "If you insist." She got her room key from the hotel clerk, and they made their way over to the elevators. "You didn't have to offer to carry my luggage."

"Hey, what are old friends for?" They stepped into the elevator. "What floor are you on?"

"Fourteen." Old friends? Camellia couldn't recall Eric saying more than fifteen words to her during the entire time in high school, and they might have exchanged four words at the reunion. She wouldn't exactly call that a friendship, but whatever.

"Looks like they skipped the thirteenth floor," Eric observed, studying the panel of elevator buttons.

"Superstitious, I guess."

He rolled his eyes. "Silly. Thirteen was always my lucky number."

The elevator stopped on the fourteenth floor, and Camellia located her room, 1407, with Eric trailing behind with her bag. "I can handle it from here," she said, as he set the suitcase in the doorway. "Thanks again."

"You're welcome," he said. She expected him to leave her alone, then, but instead he lingered. "I'll let you unpack, but if you want to meet for a drink or something later, give my room a call. I'm in 814."

"814. Got it." Camellia made a mental note of his room number, although she doubted she would call. "We'll see." Right now, more than anything, she wanted to take a shower and put other clothes on.

As Eric turned and headed back toward the elevator, though, Camellia couldn't help but admire the way his pants hugged his hips. Maybe having a drink with him would be fun. After all, they were apparently old friends now.

She closed the door behind her and drug her suitcase to the bed. She knew she had overpacked for a three-day trip—Camellia always overpacked—but now she was glad she had extra clothes. Especially if she might be entertaining former classmates for drinks. The thought made Camellia laugh as she set about unpacking. Maybe this conference wouldn't be so bad after all.

After a quick shower to cool off, Camellia dressed in pink leggings and a T-shirt which read 'Flower arranging is my therapy.' The shirt was a birthday gift from her best friend, Alison Reisetter, who was also her former therapist. She'd graduated from therapy now, so to speak, and appreciated the humor in the shirt.

Settling on the bed, Camellia decided to give Alison a call. Since it was Friday, she figured her friend would be home for the day.

"Hey," Alison greeted when she answered. "What's up? Are you in Florida?"

"Yes."

"How is it?" Alison asked.

"Hot and humid," Camellia answered. "Even worse than Texas."

"Ugh. Seriously? Okay, remind me never to go there in September," Alison said. "You'll be in air conditioning the whole time for your conference, though, right?"

"Yes, thank goodness," Camellia said. "It'll be fine. And you'll never believe who I just ran into at my hotel."

"Who?"

"Eric Grady, from high school."

"Really?" Alison's voice carried a note of surprise. "What's he doing there? Canoodling on the beach with his squeeze of the month?"

"Actually, he's emceeing at my conference," Camellia said, "as bizarre as that sounds. As for canoodling—who says that word anyway?—I'm pretty sure he's here alone, because he invited me to have a drink with him." She wasn't naïve enough to think he had a date in mind, but hey, it was an invitation, nonetheless.

"Oh, do tell," Alison said. "Specifically, tell me why you're on the phone with me when you could be with Eric Freaking Grady."

Camellia chuckled at the way her friend referred to Eric the way they'd both done in high school, back when he was the hot football star, and they were dorky girls he paid no attention to. "Because I'm not sure I'm accepting the invitation," she said. "I'm tired. It's been a long day, and the conference starts early tomorrow."

"Excuses, all of them," Alison said. "What do you have to do tomorrow besides listen to boring lectures and take occasional notes that you'll probably never look at again? I go to conferences too, you know."

"There's a little more to them in my world," Camellia said, though she declined to get into the nuances of flower conferences. Most people wouldn't get it. "You do have a point, though." She let out a sigh. "You're saying I should take him up on the invite?"

"Sure, why not? Eric was always a nice guy."

"I wouldn't know. I don't think I spoke more than twenty words to him in high school," Camellia pointed out. "And I don't think you did, either."

"No, because neither one of us traveled in his circles. Gina says he's a good guy, though." Gina Masters was their former classmate, and Alison's good friend, who had been popular back in high school. "Is he still hot?"

"Um, you just saw him two years ago at our reunion," she pointed out.

"Yes, and he was hot then, but things can change."

"In this case, they didn't," Camellia said. "He's definitely still hot."

Alison whistled. "In that case, what are you waiting for?"

"Hello... because this is me. What on earth could Eric possibly want with me?"

"Plenty, I'm sure," Alison said. "Don't sell yourself short. And hey, there's only one way to find out."

"WHAT DO ALL FLOWERS say as motivation in the morning?" Eric asked out loud, facing the mirror. "Thistle be a beautiful day."

Ugh. That one was terrible. So far, they were all terrible. He scrolled through his phone to find another joke.

"What did the flower say when her friend canceled on her at the last minute?" He smiled into the mirror. "All dressed up but nowhere to grow."

Eric groaned. Why had he ever booked this conference? He knew nothing about flowers, and he didn't even like Florida. Not since his career with the Dolphins ended so spectacularly bad.

Except he needed the closure here. That's what people told him, anyway.

Sure. Whatever. What kind of closure would there be if—when—he made a complete idiot out of himself?

The phone in his room rang, and he all but lunged to the desk to grab it. "Hello?"

"Eric? Hi, it's Camellia."

"Oh, hey." He tried to keep his tone casual and not let on how relieved he was that she called. Anything to save him from telling bad jokes to himself in front of a hotel room mirror in a city he hated and blamed for destroying his life. "What's up?"

"Not much. This is always the time at conferences when I start getting bored," she said. "Things don't get started until tomorrow. I'm too tired from traveling to go out, but not tired enough to go to sleep."

Eric found himself laughing because he'd had those same thoughts. "I hear you. There is a bar in the lobby, though," he said. "The earlier offer still stands, if you're interested."

She hesitated, but only briefly. "That's why I called. I was thinking a glass of wine sounded good, and it would probably be better with intelligent conversation," she said. "I hate talking to myself, though."

Eric laughed again. "Yeah, I know how that goes." He appreciated that she had a sense of humor, because too often the women he dated didn't. "I do it too often," he admitted. "Want to save me from myself tonight and provide the intelligent conversation if I buy your wine?"

"Yes and no," Camellia said. "I'll pay my own way, but I'll meet you in the bar in five minutes. I'll be the fat one in the flower T-shirt with the crutches."

The line went dead before Eric could reply. If he'd had the chance, though, he would've told her not to put herself down. He'd dated plenty of skinny, vapid women and they weren't all that.

Eric liked that Camellia said five minutes, not thirty or something equally ridiculous. If it meant low expectations, he was fine with that. Nowhere to go but up.

He pulled a fresh shirt from the closet and pulled it on, studying his appearance in the mirror. He might not be a hot football star anymore, but he didn't think he looked too bad, either, for forty-five. He still had most of his hair, at least.

Eric was downstairs in less than five minutes, snagging a corner table in the bar, which afforded a view of the elevator. He'd just sat down when he saw Camellia get off and headed his way.

"Hi," he said, standing as she approached. "Let me help you." He pulled out the other chair for her.

"Thanks." She sat down and removed the forearm crutches, setting them aside. "These get cumbersome at times, even if I think I rock them." Eric didn't remember those from high school and wondered what her story was, but he decided to tread lightly on that. "Have you ordered yet?"

"No. I was waiting for you," he said. "What do you like?"

"Chardonnay."

"Perfect. I'll get it." Eric made his way to the bar, ordering a glass of Chardonnay for Camellia and Merlot for himself.

"I thought I told you I'd pay my own way," she said as he set the glass in front of her.

"You did. We can still negotiate that," Eric said. "I'm not in the mood for a fight. I'm just glad you called. You saved me from telling bad jokes to myself in the mirror."

"I'm not sure I should even ask," Camellia said, chuckling

"You probably shouldn't," Eric acknowledged, but decided to try one of his jokes out on her. "What did one flower say to the other that was lost in thought?"

"A peony for your thoughts." Camellia rolled her eyes. "You probably know all of these."

"Probably, yes."

"See, you saved me from myself," Eric said. "Thank you."

"You're welcome. I sure hope you weren't planning on telling any of these tomorrow."

Chapter Two

Busted! Eric decided it was better to fess up. Own his incompetence or lack of knowledge or whatever. "Actually, I did plan on telling a joke or two, you know, just to lighten the mood," he said. "Is that a bad idea?" He usually fared well enough with jokes, but it was his first time with a group of florists.

"Not necessarily. It all depends on the joke." Camellia took drink of her wine. "I've got one for you. What is the favorite flower of a frog?"

"I have no idea."

"Croak-us," she said, laughing. "Get it?"

Eric liked her laugh, but the joke was lost on him. "No, I'm afraid I don't." He tasted his own wine and decided he approved.

"Crocus, c-r-o-c-u-s, is a seasonal flowering plant," Camellia explained. "And frogs croak."

"Right. Croak-us." Now Eric laughed, too. "I'm in way over my head. I probably should not have taken this gig." Hopefully he wasn't destined to make an idiot of himself. He'd already done that too often in the past.

"Why did you?"

"My agent thought it would be good for me." He shrugged his shoulders. "Not sure why."

"Agent?" Camellia raised an eyebrow. "Do you still work with a sports agent?"

"Oh, heck no. I left that world behind years ago and I don't plan on going back." Not that the sports world would take him back even if he wanted it to. "She's a talent and entertainment agent, and her job is to line up speaking and hosting gigs for me," Eric said. "It hasn't been a bad career, for the most part, but this one has me a bit nervous. As you can probably tell, I don't know much about flowers."

"I gathered that, yes," Camellia said. "Do you want some friendly advice from someone who does?"

"I'll take it, yeah."

"Don't try to pretend that you do," she told him. "We have presenters who are experts. We'll learn from them. So don't try too hard. Leave the corny jokes at home, or rather up in your hotel room. Just be yourself, Eric. You were always pretty darn charming back in high school." She smiled, but it was more of a half-smile. "Or so I heard, anyway. It wasn't as if we talked much."

"No, I suppose not." Eric smiled ruefully and took another drink of wine. "That was my loss, for sure."

Camellia choked out a laugh as she rolled her eyes. "See, there's that charm," she said. "And smooth flattery."

Now Eric frowned. "Do you doubt my sincerity?"

"I didn't say that."

"So, you're still making up your mind?"

After a second, Camellia nodded. "Let's go with that, yeah."

Eric chuckled. "At least I know where I stand, then." He took another drink, studying her across the table. "Are you hungry? Do you want to get something to eat?"

"Are you kidding? Fat girl here. I'm always hungry."

He ignored the fat girl comment and said, "That's something we have in common, then." He stood. "Let me see if I can round up a menu."

Eric found one on a nearby table, and they studied it, ultimately decided to share an appetizer of spinach artichoke dip and one of crab cakes. "I always feel like I should have some sort of seafood when I'm in Florida," he said. "We're so landlocked in North Texas."

"True enough," Camellia agreed. "Do you live in the Dallas area, then? I mean, I know you were at our class reunion…"

"Yeah, it's home," Eric said. "I travel a lot, though, so I frequently live out of hotels."

"Fun times." He detected sarcasm in her voice. "I go to three or four of these conferences a year, and that's enough travel for me. It's not always easy." She nodded in the direction of her crutches. "Thanks again for the assist earlier."

"Happy to help," Eric said. "What's the story behind those, anyway, if you don't mind my asking?" He didn't recall her having a disability in high school, but would he have noticed if she did? He'd been too busy running with the popular crowd.

"I wondered when you'd get around to that." Camellia took a drink of wine. "And no, I don't mind the question. I'm pretty used to it," she said. "Four years ago, I was diagnosed with multiple sclerosis. It was an aggressive case, and certainly not helped by my obesity. My doctor told me if I didn't start making some major changes, I was looking at life in a motorized scooter within a couple of years. That was quite the wake-up call, and I heeded the advice. I'm down about a hundred and ten pounds now, and hey… no scooter." She picked up one of the crutches. "As for these, I'm think I'm guilty of sometimes using them as, well, a crutch. I don't always trust my mobility or my balance, especially in unfamiliar spaces and around large groups pf people, like at conferences," she said, "but I'm working on getting better about that."

"Wow, I..." Eric wasn't sure what to say, and he was happy for the interruption of their food arriving. It gave him a second to gather his thoughts. "You look fantastic," he finally said. Sure, she was heavier than the women he was used to dating, but Camellia had bright blue eyes and a beautiful smile, and her laugh was downright infectious. Being able to have an intelligent conversation with her was an added plus, too.

"You know something, Eric?" she asked. "That actually sounded sincere, so I'll simply say thank you for the compliment."

"You're welcome, and it was sincere."

"I believe you," Camellia said, "and believe me, it's taken awhile to reach the point where I can accept a compliment from a man and not read something else into it." She eyed the food on the table. "The new, thinner me still loves food, though, so let's eat."

"I'm good with that," Eric said, and reached for a crab cake.

THEY ATE IN SILENCE for a few minutes. The dip was delicious and paired well with the wine. Camellia was glad she took Alison's advice and called Eric, because sharing appetizers and conversation with him sure beat sitting alone in her hotel room, which is what she usually ended up doing when she went to conferences.

It wasn't much different than what she used to do at home, but the last few years she'd been better about that. She still didn't date, much, but she no longer sat at home eating, watching bad movies, and being depressed, either. Now she did chair Zumba, worked in her garden, went to her weekly book club meeting, and always tried to better her craft. She loved flowers, and flowers made people happy.

"Would you like another glass of wine?" Eric asked, noticing her near empty glass.

Camellia hesitated, but only briefly. The wine was good. The company was good. And it was too early to go to sleep. "Yes, please"

"I'll be right back," he said, getting up and heading to the bar. He returned with two glasses of wine, setting one in front of her. "Chardonnay for the lady."

"Thanks."

"My pleasure." Eric sat down again. "I like your shirt, by the way."

Camellia glanced down at it. It was one of her favorites, and usually good for a few laughs. "Do you remember Alison Reisetter from high school?" she asked. "Here name was Thorne back then."

"Sure. Her daughter is dating Corey Redman's son, right?" Eric asked. "And she's friends with Gina Masters."

"That's her, yeah." Somehow, while neither Camellia or Alison had been part of the popular crowd in high school, Alison remained close friends with Gina, who'd been Homecoming Queen and Miss Popularity in Westfield's Class of 1995. "She gave me the shirt as a gift when I opened up my flower shop a few years ago," Camellia explained. "It's called 'Flower Therapy,' so the shirt fits."

"That's clever," Eric said, chuckling. "How'd you come up with it?"

"It was Alison's idea. She's a mental health counselor, and she's helped me through some difficult times in my life."

"Your MS diagnosis?"

"That, and other general lifestyle changes and adjustments, like learning to like myself, but that's another story for another time." No way was she going down that road.

"I know what you mean. I don't often like myself, either."

"You?" Camellia couldn't keep the surprise from her voice. "Mr. Popularity?"

Eric hesitated, taking a drink. "Let's just say my life hasn't always been easy, either, but that's not first date material."

"Is that what we're calling this now? A date?" She wasn't sure how she felt about that.

"That's one possible characterization," Eric said. "We can call it whatever you want, or we don't have to call it anything. Labels are overrated."

That was better. Camellia took a drink. "How about we just call it two consenting adults sharing a drink and conversation?"

"That works, too." Eric smiled, and she was struck by how handsome he was. If anything, he was better looking now that he had been in high school. Back then, she would have given anything to have a date with him. Now, she had no clue how to read his intentions here, but she had to admit she enjoyed his company.

"Alison is a good friend and she's gotten me through a lot," Camellia said, "and she helped me gain the confidence to make a lot of changes in my life, including changing careers when I left Human Resources at an insurance company to become a self-taught florist and open my own business."

"That must have taken a lot of courage," Eric said.

"Yes, but it was life changing in a very good way," Camellia said. "I know it probably sounds clichéd, but flowers bring happiness, they brighten a room, they lift people's spirits." She smiled, knowing her voice was getting more animated. It always did when she talked about her work. "So, really, they're a form of therapy." They were for her, anyway.

"Flower Therapy. I get it now," Eric said, "and I like it. You're making me glad I booked this conference after all. I'm already looking forward to learning more about your world, Camellia. And you, too."

Chapter Three

Camellia slammed her hand down against the clock on the hotel room nightstand, trying to silence the alarm. When it didn't stop after three slams, she remembered she hadn't set the alarm clock, but rather the alarm on her phone. Ugh. How pathetic was that?

She sat up and silenced the alarm.

No. She give into the negative thinking and accept herself as pathetic. She was a successful woman, and mostly strong, at least on a good day. Not pathetic at all. After all, she'd just spent the evening with Eric Freaking Grady, and he didn't seem to mind it too much. In fact, he'd even paid her a few compliments.

After a quick shower, not bothering with her hair and instead pulling it back under a ball cap sporting the name of her shop, Camellia headed downstairs for breakfast. She'd just helped herself to a blueberry muffin and coffee when someone called her name.

She turned around, recognizing a fellow florist knew from other conferences, and someone she considered a friend, even if they only saw each other a couple times a year. "Hi, Angie."

"You look great. I almost didn't recognize you."

"Thanks," Camellia said. "I'm working at it." She sat down at a table, and Angie joined her. "How's business?"

"It's been good. Prom season, followed by wedding season," her colleague said. "Those are always fun and profitable."

"Right," Camellia said. "I love the happy season." Even if she never went to her own prom or experienced her own wedding, she was still a romantic at heart.

"Me too," Angie said. "Now is the slow time, of course, but death season will be here before we know it."

Camellia laughed at her friend's remark, but it was all too true. It was well-established that more deaths occurred in January than any other month, but it was followed closely by December and February. She'd always assumed it had something to do with the winter months being gloomy and depressing. Either way, the so-called death season was a lucrative time in the flower business. "What would people think if they knew we called it that?"

"I don't know. Maybe that we're crass and morbid?" Angie mused. "Which I don't mean to be, but hey... our business has peak times, and that's one of them."

"True. I always hope for a strong prom and wedding season to sustain things until death season," Camellia said. "Which conveniently takes us to Valentine's Day." It was a holiday she'd always hated, but it was good for business.

"Yeah. It all works out." Angie bit into a muffin. "That's why I usually travel for these conferences during late summer and early fall. It's quiet at the shop."

"Same here," Camellia said. "It's good to see you again. How's your family doing?"

"They're fine. Kids are growing like weeds." Angie had two boys, and Camellia knew from her social media posts that they were active in a lot of sports. "How are you?" Angie asked. "You look happy and healthy. Is there someone in particular who might be responsible for that?"

"You mean besides me?" Camellia shook her head. "No, and that's fine with me, because I've figured out how to make my own happiness," she said. "Having a career that I love certainly helps." Sure, there were times when she got lonely, but she kept herself busy enough that those times were rare.

"Do you know if Lily is coming to this show?" Camellia asked Angie. Lily was another florist she often saw at shows, and Camellia hoped to see her again. Maybe it was because they were both named for flowers, but the two of them always shared a laugh.

'She's supposed to be. We'll probably see her in the room." Angie glanced at her watch. "Speaking of which, we should head that way so we can get good seats."

"Right." Camellia stood to throw her trash away, but Angie beat her to it, carrying it to the trash can on the other side of the room and returning before Camellia even had her crutches on. She knew Angie meant to be helpful, but the last thing Camellia needed was another reminder of her physical limitations.

"Do you need some help with your bag?" Angie asked.

"Nope. I've got it." Camellia swung it over her shoulder. "Let's go."

"I'm excited for this show," Angie said as they walked. "A two-day break from my kids and shop. Oh, and did you happen to look at the program and see the picture of the guy they have hosting this?" She whistled. "Wow."

"No," Camellia said. "didn't get a chance to look through the program yet." Normally, that would be how she spent the evening before the conference. Last night, though, she'd been too busy having wine and crab cakes with the guy in question.

"I guess he's a former football player or something. And seriously hot."

"Aren't you married?" Camellia teased her friend.

"Yes, but can still admire a good view," Angie said. "I'm sure you will, too, once you get a look at this guy."

DON'T BE AN IDIOT, and don't tell dumb jokes. That's what Eric told himself, trying to keep in mind Camellia's advice from the night before. He'd probably still make an idiot of himself. It happened more often than he cared to admit, and now he found himself in the state of Florida. That only added to the likelihood.

He should never have booked this show. Ever.

It was too late now.

Eric looked out at the room of people, mostly women, and sucked in a deep breath. What was that old adage about public speaking—you should try to envision the people in the room naked? Probably not a good idea here. When it came to women, Eric generally screwed things up. That's why he preferred to love them—in a manner of speaking—and leave them. It was far less complicated. But envisioning a room of women naked in order to break the ice?

Nope. That was not likely to be a recipe for success.

"Good morning, Miami!" He said as he approached the microphone. *I hate this city!* He thought to himself. "And welcome to the Southern Association of Florists annual conference. My name is Eric, and I'm here to make an idiot of myself in front of all of you for the next two days," he said to a round of laughter. "It's okay, though, because I'm being paid well."

More laughter. Maybe this was okay.

"What I mean by that is I know nothing about flowers. I was literally up in my room last night, standing in front of the mirror, practicing telling bad jokes about flowers."

Now, there were a few groans in the room.

Yep. Bad idea. Thankfully, Camellia had set him straight about that.

Eric surveyed the room, looking for Camellia, and finding her near the front of the room, seated at a round table with three other women. He smiled in her direction, but if she noticed, she didn't smile back.

"Fortunately, someone much wiser than me made me realize that wasn't the best way to approach things, so I promise there will be no flower jokes this morning," he said. "At least not from me," he added. "That probably leaves you wondering why I am here, and to be honest, I'm not sure myself."

Laughter again. A good sign.

"I'm not an expert on flowers, obviously. I'm a former football player. Florida State University, Class of 1999, and number one draft pick of your Miami Dolphins. It's okay if nobody remembers me, though. If you're a true Dolphins fan, you probably prefer to forget it."

There were a few laughs, but not many, and Eric wondered if they felt sorry for him. They probably should. He felt sorry for himself much of the time.

"Anyway, here I am, back in Miami. The city that ruined my life. I don't blame the city, though. It's kind of like that Jimmy Buffett song... there might a woman to blame. Or in this case, a city—okay probably a woman or three, too—but I know it's not really the city, or the women, but my own dang fault." He gave an exaggerated shrug. "These things happen though, right? I can own it."

A few more laughs. Okay, so maybe he wasn't killing it, but he wasn't dying, either. He might survive this. He needed to get off the dang stage, though.

"All right, enough about me. Let's get this party started. If you look at your agenda for the morning, you'll see there are three separate sessions to choose from to start things off—Careers in Floriculture and Horticulture, Building your Brand, and Social Media for Florists." Was there really such a thing? Apparently so. Eric was officially scared for the world.

"Choose wisely, because you never know where you might run into me."

AFTER THE ALMOST MIND-numbing session on social media, Camellia opted for a design workshop, which was much more her speed. She loved creating floral arrangements and learning new designs and techniques. It truly was a form of therapy for her. She loved flowers—the bright colors, the different species, all of it. She'd found her true calling when she opened her shop and had never looked back. Her business was successful, but she was always open to learning new things.

"That gave me a headache," Angie said from the station next to Camellia. They were each trying their hand at a new design, using repurposed items from a garden. Camellia loved gardening almost as much as she loved flowers, so this should be fun.

"What, the social media? No lie. I can barely handle Facebook on a good day," Camellia said, "and they want me to start making Tik Tok videos?" She shuddered involuntarily. "Sorry, but I am way

too old for that kind of thing, and to be honest, most of my cus-
tomers probably are, too."

"I know what you mean." Angie focused on her design of
Queen Anne's Lace and poppy mallow. "Speaking of which, did
you really go to high school with the host?"

"'Fraid so," Camellia said. After listening to her friend gush
about Eric after his opening remarks, she decided it was time to
come clean and inform Angie that she knew Eric in a previous life.

"You say that like he's a jerk or something," Angie said. "Is he?
Because I thought he came across as rather charming, in a self-dep-
recating way."

"He did," Camellia agreed. He'd obviously taken some of her
advice and skipped the awful jokes. "He is. Charming, I mean," she
said. "I don't think he's a jerk." Eric had been nothing but a gentle-
man to her the night before. "Not that I know him well. It was a big
school, and we traveled in different circles."

"You're saying you didn't date him, then?" Angie asked, and
Camellia laughed.

"Dated, no. Crushed on, yes. Not that it mattered," she said.
"Eric got around. Just not with me."

"Too bad. The hopeless romantic in me was thinking this
would be a great weekend to rekindle an old love."

"Oh, brother." Camellia rolled her eyes. "That's pushing things
even for you." She focused on her own design, filling an antique
teapot with bright summer flowers. It was exactly the type of thing
she would like to feature in her shop, if only she could put the right
Camellia-esque spin on the sample design.

They worked in relative silence for the remainder of the workshop, and Camellia ended up with a design she was happy with. It
could still be tweaked, but the potential was there, and she snapped

pictures of it with her phone so she could try her hand at recreating it when she got back home.

After the design workshop, it was time for the lunch break, and Camellia went to get box lunches for herself and her friends while Angie and Lily scoped out a shaded table on the outdoor veranda.

"Hey, Camellia, there you are."

Eric. Naturally, she'd run into him when she was carrying three lunches. "Hi," she said. "These, um, aren't all for me."

"Huh?" His eyes landed on the bags. "Oh. I didn't think they were," he said. "I guess that means you don't want to have lunch with me, then?"

"Sorry, but no. I have friends here from across the country, and usually the only time I see them is at this conference," Camellia explained. "We're eating together."

"Hey, no problem I get it," Eric said. "Tonight, then? Dinner?" he asked. "Or are you going out with your friends?"

"Actually, yes," she said. Was it her imagination, or did he look disappointed? "Why don't you join us?" Camellia was pretty sure Angie would approve.

Eric was quick to shake his head. "No, I couldn't. I'd feel too much like a third wheel," he said. "I'd like to see you again before the end of the conference, though. Can you at least promise me a drink tomorrow night at the reception following the awards dinner?"

"Are you announcing the awards?" Camellia asked.

"I am, and I'll try not to mess anything up too badly," Eric said. "So, about the drink?"

"Yes, of course," she said. "We'll have a drink." How could she turn him down when he said he wanted to see her again?

"Perfect." A grin formed on his face. "Did you happen to catch the theme for the reception?"

"No, what is it?"

"Corsages and boutonnieres," Eric said. "Fun, huh? It'll be like high school all over again."

"Oh, Lord," Camellia muttered. "Shoot me now."

Chapter Four

Two full days of workshops and seminars left Camellia exhausted, and she wasn't sure she even wanted to bother with the awards dinner, much less the reception afterward. Her book club met on Tuesday, and she still hadn't finished the book. She could order dinner and a glass of wine from room service, take a hot bath, and curl up in her jammies and read.

Now, it sounded like the perfect evening, but Camellia was all too aware that it was pretty much how she spent most of her evenings at home, minus the room service part. And she didn't fly all the way to Miami to sit in her hotel room and read.

The night before, she'd enjoyed a fun girls' night out with Angie and Lily. They were good friends, but also friends she only saw once or twice a year when she traveled to conferences. If she bailed on the dinner tonight, she'd gave up an opportunity to spend more time with them.

And then there was the whole Eric thing, too. Camellia hadn't spoken to him since running into him before lunch the day before, but she had promised him a drink tonight. She didn't want to go back on her word. Besides, she was flattered he wanted to spend more time with her, even if she was reluctant to read anything into it.

She stood in front of the closet, studying the clothes she brought, trying to decide what to wear. Since she always overpacked for these trips, there were plenty of options, but that didn't mean any appealed to her.

The room extension rang, and Camellia went to answer it, assuming it might be a check-out reminder for tomorrow. "Yes?"

"Camellia, it's Eric. What are you wearing?"

"Excuse me?" Her jaw might have dropped, but since she wasn't looking in the mirror, she couldn't be sure. "Are we jumping right to phone sex? Because I'd hoped for a little foreplay beforehand."

"What? Jesus, that came out wrong," he said.

"Yeah, maybe." Still, Camellia couldn't pass up the chance to play along. "At the moment, I'm not wearing anything but my underwear," she said, "while I try to figure out what to wear for the reception."

"Please, don't tempt me with that image," Eric said.

Camellia choked out a laugh. "I rather doubt the image of me half-naked would tempt you to do anything but run," she said. "Why did you call, Eric?"

"I'm fairly certain you're wrong on that," he replied, "but I actually called to find out if you were wearing a specific color tonight."

Huh. Interesting. Camellia stretched the phone as far as it would reach, trying to get back over to the closet. Why didn't they put cordless phones in these rooms, anyway? Probably because they figured no one ever used them. "Why?" she asked.

"So, I can get you a corsage," Eric said. "Keeping up with the theme, you know?"

"Oh. Right." Camellia bit back a sarcastic remark, because it was kind of a sweet gesture, and if she closed her eyes, maybe it would all seem a little bit fulfilling one of her high school fantasies.

"Go with blue," she said, with a glance back in the closet. It wasn't a favorite color of hers, but she had a pair of blue capris and a white and blue printed shirt that she didn't look too much like a whale in. If anyone, including Eric, thought she was wearing a dress, they had something else coming.

"Blue?" He repeated.

"That's what I said."

"Perfect. It's my favorite color," Eric said. "I'll wear my blue tie."

"Fabulous." Why did he insist on talking about this like it was a date or something? Was it all an attempt to torture her? "I've got to get ready and meet my friends," Camellia said, "but feel free to look for me after the awards dinner if you're serious about that drink."

"Of course, I'm serious. Why would you think otherwise?" He asked. "I'm even getting you a corsage."

"Perfect, then. I can't wait to see it." Camellia took the phone back to its rightful place on the nightstand before returning to the closet and grabbing her clothes off the hanger. She was still confused, even a little bit wary, of Eric's intentions, but she promised him blue, so she'd wear blue.

Twenty minutes later, she was downstairs in the reception hall, where Angie and Lily had thankfully saved her a seat at table with a few other industry professionals they knew. "Sorry I'm late," Camellia said, sitting down. "I got a phone call."

"Nothing's wrong, I hope," Lily said, her expression concerned.

"Not at all. Just our host for the evening wondering about my choice in attire." She rolled her eyes. "I promised him a drink after dinner, and I guess he thinks that means I need a corsage," Camellia said. "I told him blue, and he said he'd wear a blue tie."

"That's sweet," Lily said.

"It's... interesting." Camellia looked to her friends. "Are you staying for the reception?"

"Not me," Lily said. "I have an early morning flight and need to pack."

"I am," Angie said. "One more night away from the kids and the hubby? I'll be dancing the night away, probably with a fruity-colored drink in my hand."

"Perfect. Then you can join Eric and me for a drink."

"Thanks, but no thanks," Angie said. "He's certainly hot, but I wouldn't want to intrude upon your reunion with your high school crush."

"Oh, please." Camellia rolled her eyes. "It's one drink, and probably a bad idea. More than likely, I'll be upstairs in my room reading by 8:45."

ERIC WAS MORE THAN happy to wrap up the awards dinner, thereby ending his duty as the host of the Southern Association of Florists annual conference. It hadn't been a bad gig. Actually, he thought it had gone fairly well, especially for a guy who didn't know much of anything about flowers. He didn't think he'd made a complete fool of himself, anyway.

He was ready to be off duty, though, and be able to have that drink with Camellia.

The association president cornered him on his way to the cash bar. "Eric, thank you again. You did a wonderful job."

"Thank you for the opportunity, Ms. Smithson. I enjoyed it," he said. "I worried I might be in over my head, but hopefully that didn't show too much." Eric shrugged. "Or if it did, it came across as charming."

Paula Smithson laughed. "I have little doubt about that," she said. "I'm taking a few days off after this, but it won't be long before I get to work planning next year's conference. Shall I contact your agent about booking?"

They wanted him back? Just like that? "Um, yes. Rochelle handles everything for me. So far, I think next year is still pretty open, but if you're serious, go ahead and put in the request." He tried to make it sound as if he were in great demand but didn't know if he succeeded.

"I'll do that."

"Wonderful. I'll certainly give it careful consideration if the dates work out," Eric said. "If you'll excuse me, Ms. Smithson..."

"Please, call me, Paula," she said. "And yes, of course, I have to make the rounds, but if you're free a little later..."

"Sorry, but most likely not." Eric wasn't sure what he was turning down and didn't much care. "I ran into an old friend from high school here, and I sort of promised her a drink," he said. "And a corsage."

Was it his imagination, or did Paula appear disappointed? "Okay, then. I won't keep you," she said. "Hopefully, I'll have you back here next year. Thank you, Eric."

He exhaled in relief as Paula took her leave and hurried over to the stand where the corsages were being sold. "I need something blue, please."

"Do you have a particular flower in mind?"

"What? No. Blue," Eric said. "Whatever you recommend." Were there that many blue flowers? Apparently so, but after a few minutes of deliberation, he settled for a corsage of blue poppies. He doubted it would be the right shade of blue to match whatever

Camellia was wearing, but it would have to do. It was pretty, anyway.

With the corsage in hand, he went in search of her. The banquet room had quickly transitioned to a dance hall, with colored lighting and a cash bar, but he didn't spot Camellia on the dance floor, instead finding her seated at a corner table by herself.

"Hey, sorry to keep you waiting," he said as he approached the table. "I got waylaid by my boss for the weekend."

"And who would that be?"

"The SAF president, Paula Smithson," Eric said, sitting down next to her. "I think she might've hit on me." Maybe?

"Of course." Camellia rolled her eyes. "Occupational hazard, I'm sure."

Eric frowned. "What's that supposed to mean?"

"Just that I assume you probably get hit on a lot," she said.

"Not as much you might think," Eric said. "Anyway, I told her I already had a date." He set the corsage on the table in front of her. "I got you this, as promised. I hope it's the right color blue."

"It's pretty close." Camellia smiled as she slipped it on her left wrist. "Thank you. I wasn't sure you were serious about the whole corsage thing, and I thought it was kind of dumb at first..."

"Yeah, you didn't seem too impressed with the idea when I called your room earlier."

"No, because it's a little too high schoolish for me," she said. "And that's not a good thing, because I hated high school."

"What?" Eric asked. "You can't be serious. Nobody hates high school. It was the best time of our lives."

"Yours, maybe," Camellia said. "You were the golden boy. Mr. Popularity. It was a great time for you. Me, not so much." She twirled her arm around, admiring the corsage. "This is the first one of these I've ever gotten."

"Are you serious?"

"I am," Camellia said.

He blinked. "Are you saying you never went to homecoming?"

"No. I did go, senior year," she said. "Alison was my date."

"What?"

"Just what I said. Alison was my date. Neither one of us had an actual date, and we didn't want to miss out on the experience, being out senior year and all, so went together." Camellia shrugged. "We had a decent time, even if most people assumed we were a couple and snickered behind our backs."

"Oh, jeez," Eric said. "That must've been weird."

"Maybe a little, since we were seventeen at the time," she said. "But, seriously, Alison's awesome. If we were both lesbians, we could do a lot worse, right?"

"I, um..." He had no idea what to say. "I suppose?"

Camellia laughed. "Good answer. Are you going to get me that drink now? The one you promised?"

"I am." Eric stood. "Chardonnay, right?"

"Yes. Thanks for remembering."

"Back in a flash." He got up and made his way to the cash bar, ordering their drinks, while still taking in what Camellia said. He knew they didn't have the same circle of friends in high school but assumed her experience couldn't have been that much different from his. After all, high school was high school, right? He'd assumed it more or less the same for everyone, but apparently that was the naïve way of thinking.

"Here you go," he said, setting the drink in front of her. "I'm sorry if this is awkward." He thought the whole corsage thing would be fun, but maybe not.

"What? You finally realizing that not everyone loved high school the way you did?"

"Maybe. Sort of." Because for him, it had been the best time of his life. "It really wasn't good for you?"

"Not even close, but I'm open to reconsideration if you can prove I was wrong." She studied the corsage on her wrist. "You got me this, after all. And wine."

Chapter Five

"Wine is always a plus, right?" Eric asked. He found himself a little out of his element here as he studied his glass. Did anyone truly hate high school?

Apparently, Camellia did.

"The wine is excellent, yes," she said. "Had there been wine in high school, I'm sure it would have been infinitely more bearable."

"Come on, you had to like something about it."

"Well, let's see. Mr. Miller's AP English Lit was pretty good," she said. "I enjoyed reading Invisible Man."

"You did?"

He must've have sounded surprised, because Camellia responded with, "Why? Didn't you?"

"Oh, I totally did," Eric said. "I just assumed I was the only one."

"No, it was a popular read, at least among me and my dorky friends," Camellia told him. "Maybe that was the problem? You were far too concerned about being popular, and hanging with the 'in' crowd that you didn't want to admit you actually enjoyed reading a hella long book published in the 1950s?"

Eric simply stared at her for a minute before taking a drink of his wine. "Nail. Head. Direct hit," he finally said. "Wow. You're good."

"Was it difficult? Being Mr. Popularity, the hotshot quarterback, Homecoming King and all that?" she asked. "I always figured it would be. So many expectations to live up to." Camellia shrugged. "In that regard, maybe it was better being the chubby girl nobody liked. I mean, zero expectations there."

There was so much to take from her words, Eric didn't even know where to begin? Had her self-esteem really been that low? And how did she get to be so perceptive about his own experience, since hers had apparently been the opposite? "I was never Homecoming King," he said. "I was the Prince. Corey was King, because everything he touched came up golden. I used to call him Midas."

"You're serious? You were jealous of Corey?" Camellia asked. "You were the quarterback of the football team. And we won state."

"Yeah, but Corey got the girl." And everything else.

"Which one do you mean? Gina, or Brittany? Because he dumped Gina for Brit before graduation. Then divorced Brit for Gina. I mean, not exactly, but close," she said.

"It wasn't about either of them," Eric said. "Just a... thing. It probably sounds weird, but it always seemed like Corey had it all together, and I didn't come close."

"Yeah, because winning the Texas high school state championship, then winning the national championship your senior year at Florida State, and then being drafted number one overall by the Dolphins was just nothing," Camellia said. "It's a shame your life has been so awful, Eric."

Zing! He wanted to say, 'If only you knew,' but he wasn't sure he wanted to delve into that depressing saga right now.

Instead, Eric shook his head. "I never said it was awful." Her reaction was proof people only saw the superficial, though. "But not as easy as people think," he said. "You know I got drafted by the Dolphins. Do you remember what happened after that?"

"Sorry, no. I crushed on you all through high school, but you didn't have time for me. Still, I followed your career through college," Camellia said. "Old habits and all, but after that my own life kind of changed course, rather unexpectedly, and you were no longer my top priority."

"Fair enough." Eric exhaled. "It's just as well because it wasn't pretty. Let's face it, there's a reason I'm emceeing flower conferences and not working on my pro football Hall of Fame speech."

"I suppose." Camellia took a drink of wine. "Do you want to tell me what happened? Because I honestly don't know," she said, "although you kind of hinted at something in your remarks yesterday. About this city."

"Yeah." Eric smiled wryly. "I hate the city, but I think it hated me first." He drained his glass of wine. "I'll give you the Cliffs Notes version. Got drafted by the Dolphins as the heir apparent to Marino. I was going to be a superstar. Then I blew out my knee in the second game of the season against the Patriots. ACL, LCL, MCL. Name a ligament and I tore it up. I mean, why do anything halfway?"

"I'm sorry. That must've been awful."

"It was worse than that, but the pain meds helped," Eric said. "They were my salvation, but also my undoing."

"Are you saying you became addicted?"

"Yep. You wouldn't believe how easy it is." He raked a hand through his hair. "Society loves to bash substance abusers, though, rather than trying to understand. There's so much stigma."

"No kidding. Why do you think I rely on these so much," Camellia gestured to one of her crutches, "whenever I'm with a crowd or in unfamiliar places?" she asked. "Given two bad choices, I'd rather be looked at as handicapped rather than have people see me stumbling around and assuming I'm drunk or on drugs."

"See, you get it." Eric leaned back in his seat, studying her face. She really was pretty and found himself wishing he would've noticed her in high school. Then maybe she wouldn't have had to go to the Homecoming dance with Alison and have everyone assume they were gay. "So, um, would you like to dance?"

Camellia choked on her wine as she swallowed. "You cannot be serious."

"I was, a little, but I can adjust." Eric nodded in the direction of her nearly empty glass. "I can get you another glass of wine, and we'll sit here and watch people and lament the bad things that have happened to us over the past twenty-eight years," he said. "Or we can get a whole bottle and take it up to my room. I hope I don't have to tell you which I prefer."

CAMELLIA BLINKED AND stared at her Eric, unsure if she'd heard him correctly.

"Well?" He asked expectantly. "Which is it going to be?"

Don't read too much into this. He just wants to talk, maybe relive a little of his glory years. After all, she was the one who pried and made him come clean about his struggles in the NFL. Even if she did only get the Cliffs Notes version.

"I'll go with option B," Camellia said, standing up. "Let me just say goodbye to friend Angie, in case I don't get back down here." And she didn't expect to get back down here. She'd have another glass of wine, maybe two, with Eric, and then she'd head up to her own room to pack.

"Perfect. You do that while I see if I can finagle a full bottle of wine from someone."

"Oh, I have faith. If anyone can, you can."

Eric sauntered off in the direction of the bar, while Camellia went in search of Angie, who was making good on her promise to dance the night away. "I'm heading upstairs," she said, when she managed to drag Angie away from the dance floor. "I wanted to say goodbye, though."

"Upstairs?" Angie asked. "To your room, or Eric's?"

"His," Camellia admitted. "Don't read too much into that, though. We're just talking."

"Are you sure about that?" Angie raised an eyebrow.

Camellia was no longer sure of anything, at least as far as Eric was concerned, but she wasn't ready to admit that, so she ignored her friend's pointed question. "Have a safe trip back to Michigan," she said. "I'll see you here next year?"

"You know I wouldn't miss it. Safe travels to you, too. And I wish you a very successful death season."

Camellia let out a laugh. What would people think if they knew what a morbid group florists could be? "You too, Ang." They exchanged a hug before Angie returned to the dance floor, swiveling her hips to the beat of the music.

Eric stood on the doorway of the ballroom, clutching a bottle of wine and two glasses. "Success!" he declared, raising the bottle.

"I don't even want to know what you paid for that."

"No, you probably don't." They took the elevator to the eighth floor, and Eric handed her the bottle while he used his keycard to unlock the door. "I got the Chardonnay like you like."

"Thanks." She didn't want to tell him he probably should've gotten what he liked, since she was only having one more glass before retiring to her own room.

Camellia walked into his room and looked around, trying to be subtle about it. She found that she couldn't because it surprised her how neat and orderly it was. A few shirts hung in the closet, and his suitcase—fully zipped—lay on the luggage stand. There was a laptop computer on the desk, but the screen was closed. Her own hotel room was the total opposite, with clothes and conference materials strewn on the bed she wasn't using.

"I'm kind of a neat freak," Eric said, as if reading her thoughts. "Something I picked up in rehab."

So, he had gone through rehab. Camellia had questions, plenty of them, but she didn't know if they'd be welcome. Probably not, she decided, when Eric handed her a glass of wine. "Thanks," she said, noticing it was filled to the rim.

"Shall we toast?" he suggested, raising his own equally full glass. "To new beginnings and old friends."

"Sure, whatever." She touched her glass to his, trying to be careful not to spill any of the wine. "Except we were never friends."

"You keep pointing that out." Eric walked over to the King bed and laid back on it. "My bad. I'm trying to rectify that, okay?"

"If you say so." There was a chair by the window, and Camellia sat in it.

"I like you, Camellia," he said. "If I'd been smart enough to get to know you in high school, I probably would've liked you then, too. I don't know." He drained his glass in a few big gulps and refilled it. "I've never been all that bright."

"Yet you took AP English and enjoyed Invisible Man," she reminded him.

"Shh." He held a finger to his lips. "That can't get out. I have an image to protect, you know."

"See, that's your problem." Camellia took a drink, or three, from her glass. "You care too much what people think of you."

"Are you saying you don't?" He countered.

It wasn't an easy question. If Alison were here, in her therapist hat, she'd undoubtedly tell Camellia she still cared, too, even if she tried to insist otherwise. "Sometimes. I'm getting better, though," she said. "Don't hog all that wine, okay?" She took the bottle from the nightstand and refilled her own glass.

"You can join me on the bed, you know," Eric said. "It's big, and I don't bite."

Camellia arched a brow and sat down on the bed "You sure about that?"

"Only if you ask me to." He gave her a mischievous smile, and she was pretty sure her heart rate increased.

"Oh." She turned her head to look out the window, which afforded a view of the parking lot.

"Can I ask you a question?" Eric asked.

"I don't bite, either."

"Sucks to be me." He laughed. "I was actually going to ask you about your name," he said. "Were you named after the flower?"

"You know it's a flower? I'm impressed, Eric," Camellia said. "And yes, it's the state flower of Alabama."

"Are you from there? Alabama?"

"I am. Born in Greenville, which is known the Camellia City," she said. "I'm surprised you couldn't tell from my accent, because it's not North Texas."

"So, how'd you end up there?" Eric asked. "In Westfield?"

"My dad's job. I've always considered myself a 'Bama girl, though, so as soon as I graduated, I headed home for college."

"Roll Tide?"

Camellia shook her head. "War Eagle."

"Interesting. Yet you ended up back in Texas."

"Yes, but that's a long story."

"One you don't want tell," Eric surmised.

"Not really, no," she said. "Not tonight, anyway."

"Then we'll move on," he said. "Does anyone call you Cami?"

"No, never."

"Do you mind if I do?"

Camellia considered it for a moment and shrugged. "I suppose not."

"Then Cami it is." Eric smiled. "You're very agreeable tonight."

"It's probably the wine." Camellia glanced at her nearly empty glass. She'd end up with a headache, but she didn't care.

"What would you say if I told you I think you're beautiful and I'd really like to kiss you?"

"I'd say 'You're drunk, Eric.'"

"Not quite, but I'm getting there." He moved closer to her, his face merely inches away from hers, and Camellia closed her eyes.

She wanted to tell him he was twenty-eight years too late., but when his lips met hers, none of that seemed to matter. Besides, he was probably a better kisser now than he had been at seventeen, anyway.

"Eric." His name came off her lips in a breathless whisper as they reluctantly parted, coming up for air. Okay, he was almost certainly a better kisser now.

"What? Is this the part where you say this would be a mistake, and we'd both end up regretting it?"

"No. This is the part where I say what happens in Miami, stays in Miami."

Chapter Six

Camellia woke up a with a dry mouth, a splitting headache, and a full bladder, and sat up in bed to try to orient herself to her surroundings. Was she back in college? No. She could handle the effects of alcohol a lot easier at twenty-one, and this sure wasn't her dorm back at Auburn University.

Florida. She was in Florida. In Eric's hotel room.

She glanced over at the other side of the bed, where Eric lay sprawled out on the bed, face down. He was there. She didn't imagine it.

The empty bottle of wine sat on the table beside the bed, along with the two empty glasses, the evidence of their questionable decision-making.

Camellia knew better—or ought to know better—than to drink that much, but the wine was good, the company was better, and besides, this was a vacation of sorts, even if it was, technically, a work trip.

She located her discarded shirt from the floor and pulled it on before making her way to the bathroom. She didn't care to look at her naked self in the mirror while she was in there. After taking care of business, she filled a plastic cup with water from the sink and drank it down in one gulp. She wished she had something to take for her head, but she wasn't in her own room.

Camellia studied the stuff Eric had spread out on the bathroom vanity but didn't see any pain relievers. The discarded condoms and wrappers were there, though, in the wastebasket on the floor, so she hadn't imagined that either.

She had sex with Eric Freaking Grady. Twice.

She filled the cup with water again.

"Camellia? Are you still here?"

"Yes. I'll be out in second," she called back, drinking the water before opening the door.

He sat on the edge of the bed, his eyes bleary from sleep and his golden-brown hair mussed. "I was afraid maybe you left."

"Nope. I was snooping to see if you had any Advil or Tylenol. I've got a bit of a headache."

"Sorry, but no. I don't take any of that stuff anymore."

"It's oke—" The thought left her as her eyes landed on Eric's impressive morning wood. "Oh," she managed to say, not trusting herself to string more words together.

"Right. Jesus." He pulled the sheet over his lap. "I should put something on."

"No, you shouldn't," she said. "Lay back down." Wherever this confidence came from, Camellia didn't know, nor did she know how long it might last. While she had it, though, she might as well have a little fun.

"What are you do—" He stopped mid-word as she straddled him.

"Do you have any condoms left?"

"Yes. Here." Eric reached over to the nightstand and retrieved one, handing it to her. "Are you sure... I mean, can you..."

Camellia inwardly winced. This was not the time or place for questions about any handicap she might have. "Shut up, Eric, and

I'll show you what I can do," she said, lowering herself onto him. "How's this?"

"Perfect. I want to look at you, though. Take your shirt off."

The night before, she'd insisted on turning off the lights. Now, with the bright sun streaming through the window, she couldn't him. The confidence hadn't left her yet, though, so she pulled the shirt over her head, tossing it to the floor.

"God, you're beautiful," Eric said.

"I think that's more a reflection of the position I currently have you in, but I'll go with it," she said as she began to move on him.

And hoped she wouldn't colossally embarrass herself.

No. Don't think about that.

Camellia banished the thought from her head, increasing her tempo as she rode Eric to his climax.

"Oh, God. Sweet Jesus, Cami."

Last night, when he'd given her the nickname, Camellia wasn't sure if she liked it. Hearing it in the throes of passion, she decided she did. "I didn't know you were a religious man," she joked, falling on top of him.

She didn't know how long she laid there before Eric asked, "Are you okay? Can you move?"

Oh, right. She should do that. "I... think so." Camellia sat up and tried to move off him. "Hold on."

"I can't exactly go anywhere until you do," Eric pointed out.

So much for not embarrassing herself. It would be okay, though. After this, Camellia doubted she would ever see Eric again.

She rolled on to her back, managing not to hit him with her knee. Not graceful, but it worked. "Sorry about that."

"Don't be sorry. That was incredible."

"Aside from the beached whale on top of you, you mean?"

Eric shook his head. "No, Cami, that wasn't what I meant at all."

Camellia ignored that and located her discarded bra and shirt. Somewhere, she had pants, too. If she could find those, she could go back to her own room, shower, and pack. "I have to get ready to leave for the airport."

"What time's your flight to Dallas?" Eric asked.

"Twelve fifteen."

"Mine, too. We're probably on the same flight," he said. "Small world, huh?"

"Yeah." Sometimes it was too small.

"Do you mind giving me a lift to the airport? I don't have a car here and I got a little distracted last night and forgot to reserve a shuttle."

"Sure. I'll give you a ride." She found her pants. "Meet you in the lobby in forty-five minutes?" That would give her enough to take a quick shower and pack.

"How about I come up to your room? I can help you get your bags down."

Camellia wanted to say no, she could do it herself. But of course, she couldn't. "Fine."

NOTHING LIKE GOING from hot sex to glacial coldness in under an hour. Eric officially didn't understand women at all. Not this one, anyway.

He offered to drive Camellia's rental car to the airport, and she snapped at him, insisting she could drive just fine.

She could, but the drive proved to be a tense and quiet one. Eric made a few attempts at conversation, but Camellia didn't seem interested. She said few words and barely glanced his way, instead concentrating on the road.

Since carrying on a conversation was apparently not going to happen, Eric was left to try to figure out where things had gone awry. Sure, they'd had too much wine the night before, and Camellia woke up with a headache, but she said it was gone now—he managed to elicit that much of a response from her.

As for the sex, it was spectacular. When he'd woken up this morning and found the other side of the bed empty, Eric had feared the worst—that Camellia regretted their night together and had slipped out of his room in the middle of the night so she wouldn't have to see him again. That was something Eric had never experienced—usually he was the one doing the leaving.

But no, she was still there, and had even gone full cowgirl on him. That didn't exactly scream regret to Eric, so why the cold treatment all the sudden? He didn't get it.

"Are you upset with me about something?" he dared to ask once they had navigated their way through security and located their departure gate.

"No. Why would you think that?"

"I don't know. You're awfully quiet." She'd been anything but quiet the night before. She'd been talkative, witty and, well, sexy, as hell.

"Sorry. It's not you. I'm just not looking forward to the flight home," Camellia said. "I told you that traveling—walking through airports, sitting on airplanes—isn't easy for me."

She had, and he understood it was difficult. Camellia was a proud woman who didn't like to ask for help or be dependent on others for assistance. She'd accepted his help when they left the hotel, and again as they made their way through the airport terminal, but Eric could sense she wasn't happy about it.

"I know, but at least it's a direct flight," Eric said, "and only about two and a half hours."

"True." Camellia managed a smile; the first one Eric had seen since she left his hotel room. "It could be worse."

"Do you have a car parked at DFW, or is someone picking you up?"

"My car is there," she said.

"Perfect. Then I'll give you a hand with your stuff when we land."

"My good Samaritan."

Eric shrugged, trying to downplay the compliment. "It's something any decent guy would do." Maybe Camellia wasn't used to decent guys, though. "What seat are you in?"

She glanced at her boarding pass. "Seventeen F."

"Hmm. I'm a few rows back, but I'll see if I can switch."

"You don't have to do that."

"No, but maybe I want to. Be right back." He got up and walked over to see the gate agent. Since the flight wasn't full, she was able to accommodate his request.

"You're in luck," he told Camellia when he returned to their seats. "Or rather I am." He grinned. "I got moved to Seventeen E. Isn't that great?"

"I hope you don't expect me to join the mile high club with you, Eric," Camellia said, "because I used up all my limber moves this morning."

She smiled as she said it, and Eric relaxed. Maybe things were okay, after all. "That's all right, because trust me, those are moves I will remember for a very long time."

When they boarded the plane, Eric helped place her carry-bag and crutches in the overhead bin, but when he tried to help Camellia with the seat belt extender, she pushed his hand away.

"I'm not helpless," she said, snapping it in the place.

"Far from it. I think you're incredibly strong. I guess it's just my nature to want to help," he said. "I didn't mean to offend you."

"It's fine." Camellia pulled a book from her purse. "You can stop being nice to me, though. I already slept with you."

"Whoa, where did that come from?" Just when he thought things were okay again. "Are you saying you regret last night?"

"Regret?" She shook her head. "Not at all. It was great, but let's not make it something more than it was. It was good sex, fueled by a lot of good wine, and it was a very pleasant, if unexpected, way to end the conference," she said. "We're going home now, though. You can go back to your skinny, super model girlfriend of the week. Month. Whatever. And forget about me."

"Wow." It took a few seconds for the words, and their apparent implication, to sink in. "You have this all figured out, don't you?"

"I think so, yes," she said. "And please, wipe the cocky grin off your face. You got another notch on your belt, or bedpost, or whatever it is."

Eric made a point of running his hand over his face and adopting a serious expression. "Okay, a couple things here. One, I don't have a girlfriend back home, skinny, model or otherwise. If I did, I would not have been with you last night. I don't know what you think you know about me, but that's not how I roll. And two, I have no intention of forgetting about you, not that I think that would be possible, anyway. I'll decide how I proceed with things from here, with your express permission and willingness, of course, but regardless of your level of interest, I won't forget about you or pretend last night didn't happen."

He took a deep breath. "Three—"

"There's three now? I thought you said a couple."

"I changed my mind, but we can call this two, subsection b, if you prefer. I like you, Cami. A lot. You're witty and smart and lots of fun, and I think you're beautiful, too." Eric smiled. "Just a little something for you to think about for the next two and a half hours."

"Are you done, now?"

"Yep." He nodded his head, still grinning. "Now I am."

"Great. Because I have to finish reading this before my book club meets on Tuesday." She turned away from him, her eyes focused on the book, but Eric could see she was smiling. That was good enough for now.

He grabbed the airline magazine from the seat back pocket and stretched his legs out.

Chapter Seven

Eric left her alone for the duration of the flight, leaving Camellia plenty of time to read her book and to think about what he said. Even if she didn't want to think about it, it was darn near impossible not to. He'd gotten to her, plain and simple, and she wasn't sure how to react.

When they landed in Dallas, Camellia was prepared to ask for assistance from airport staff, but Eric would have none of it, wheeling her suitcase and his own on the trek to her car.

"You haven't mastered the art of packing light, have you?"

"No, sorry." She gave him a sheepish smile. "It's not too much further. I've got prime parking," she said. "Handicap tag." She didn't always use it. She didn't want to think of herself as handicapped. But when it came to parking at the Dallas-Ft. Worth airport, Camellia didn't hesitate to use that tag.

"And here we are," she said when she located her burgundy Kia Telluride. "This is Rosie." Camellia pressed the button to unlock her car and opened the hatch.

"She's pretty." Eric lifted Camellia's suitcase inside. "Do you have a long drive home?"

Camellia shook her head. "No. I live up in Flower Mound," she said, referring to the northwest Dallas suburb. "Twenty minutes from the airport, and only five from my shop."

"That's nice and convenient."

"Yes, and you are not escorting me home," Camellia said. "Just putting that out there."

Eric laughed. "I know that. Just making conversation," he said. "Can I see your phone for a second?"

She hesitated, briefly, before entering her passcode and handing it to him.

He tapped at the screen, and his phone rang from inside his pocket. After two rings, he ended the call and handed the phone back to her. "There. The last number you called was me," Eric said. "So, when I call you—and that is when, not if—you'll know who it is, and you can decide whether to answer. You can also call me," he added, "if you're so inclined."

"Or block you?"

"Ouch. Your words wound me, but I'm a confident man, nonetheless." Eric closed Rosie's hatch. "Drive safely."

"You, too." Camellia watched him walk away before unlocking her phone again. She went to the last number called and added Eric to her contacts.

Once she was in her car and her phone linked to the Bluetooth, she placed a call. Not to Eric, but to Alison.

She answered on the second ring. "Hey. Are you back in town?"

"Yep. I'm just leaving the airport. Are you at home?"

"Where else would I be on a Sunday afternoon? Bret's watching the Cowboys game, and I'm cleaning the house," Alison said. "Fun times."

Cleaning. Camellia had to clean her house, too, but she also wanted to talk to her friend. "Do you mind if I swing by for a little bit?"

"Not at all. You can even stay for dinner if you want. It's kind out of your way, though." Alison and Bret lived in Plano, on the other side of the Metroplex. "Is something wrong?"

"Nope. All good," Camellia said as she exited the airport parking lot. "I'll see you in half an hour, assuming traffic isn't too bad."

Thirty-two minutes later, Camellia pulled into the drive of Bret and Alison's house and her friend met her at the front door. "Are you sure nothing's wrong? You got me worried."

"You're sweet, but I'm fine," Camellia insisted as they went in the house. "I could use a glass of wine, though, if you have any?"

"Already chilling." Alison took a bottle out of the refrigerator. "Like I said, you got me worried. Now, will you tell me what's going on?"

"I slept with Eric."

ERIC PASSED THE EXIT for Flower Mound as he drove on to Lewisville, the suburb he called home, and thought of Camellia. Not that he'd stopped thinking about her since he bumped into her in the parking lot of the hotel in Miami. Now she expected him to simply forget about her? That was so not happening.

It was weird to think they both still lived within twenty miles of where they'd gone to high school together, yet it took a trip to Florida for a garden conference for their paths to cross. Maybe it shouldn't have been, though. After all, there had been 632 people in their graduating class and more than six million lived in the greater Dallas-Ft. Worth metroplex. Maybe the weird part was that anyone ever ran into the same person twice without seeking them out. It had to be up to chance or something.

Well, screw chance. They were practically neighbors, and Eric fully intended to see more of Camellia. To do that, though, he had to convince her that he was worth her time.

He stared the media screen in his car. He had her phone number now, so she was one touch away, in a matter of speaking. And since Camellia lived closer to the airport, she was probably already home.

Should he do it?

No. It was too aggressive. Eric didn't want to risk angering her or scaring her off. He'd waited this long to find a woman he wanted to spend more time with, even after he'd already slept with her. He could certainly wait another day or two.

Okay, not two. That was pushing it. He'd call tomorrow.

With a plan, a goal, and a purpose, Eric smiled as he pulled into the driveway of his two-story brick home that looked remarkably like every other one on the block. One builder, two brick colors, three floor plans. Was it any wonder they were all cookie cutter houses?

As he stopped the car and stepped out, his neighbor, Tess, came out of her house to greet him. She'd probably been sitting in her living room, looking out the front window, waiting for him to get home so she could pounce. Tess was twelve years older, widowed the year before, and made no secret of her interest in Eric. So far, he hadn't taken the bait.

"Eric!" Tess waved as she hurried over. "How was your trip?"

"Much better than I expected," he said. "How are things here? How's my girl?"

"Lizzie's fine," Tess said. "She spent most of the time over here with me and Chloe, but I took her back over to your house a little bit ago so she could run around her own backyard. I think she was getting homesick, and I knew you'd be back soon."

"Thanks, Tess."

"She's probably ready for a walk."

"I'm on it as soon as I get my stuff inside." Eric retrieved his suitcase from the trunk. "I appreciate you looking after her and keeping an eye on house, too." Tess was a huge help whenever he had to travel. It was one reason—not the only one—that he'd never slept with her. When things went wrong, as they inevitably would, he didn't want to lose her as a friend and reliable dog-sitter.

"Do you want company for the walk?" Tess asked. "Or dinner later?"

Eric almost felt sorry for her. She was a nice lady, not at all unattractive, and he knew she was lonely. It was too easy, though, and he feared there would be too many strings. "I'm going to take a rain check, Tess," he said, hoping to let her down gently. "I'm tired from traveling, and I don't think I'd be very good company tonight. I'm just going to take my girl for a walk, watch a little football and go to bed early."

"All right." His neighbor didn't try to hide her disappointment. "If you change your mind, though..."

"I'll call. I promise." They both knew he wouldn't.

He wheeled his suitcase up the front walk and unlocked the door. He'd no sooner pushed it open and yelled, "Lizzie, Daddy's home," when the yellow lab came running. "Ah, there's my girl," Eric said, bending down to give her a hug as she licked at his face. "I missed you." He stood up. "Tess said you're antsy for a walk, so let me just grab your leash."

His phone buzzed, and Eric pulled it from his pocket, hoping the text might be from Camellia, but no such luck. Instead, it came from one of his semi-regular hook-ups, wanting to, well, hook up.

Not happening.

Sorry, not tonight, he replied, though he wasn't sorry at all.

"What do you say, Liz?" Eric asked as he attached the leash to her collar. "Shall we delete Keely from our contacts? Bark one for yes."

When the dog barked once and stopped, Eric smiled. "Smart girl. I think so, too." With a single swipe, Keely was gone, but there would be more to follow. Eric spoke the truth when he told Camellia he didn't have a girlfriend at home. It wasn't the entire truth, though because there were always women available for no strings sex.

No longer, though. Eric was going to walk Lizzie and then have a beer while he purged his contact list. It was well past time to do that.

"SO, ANYWAY, THE TAKEAWAY from this is that cowgirl is not the best position for a woman of my considerable size, and with limited flexibility," Camellia said, finishing recounting the story for Alison.

Naturally, her friend was laughing.

Camellia glared at her. "I'm glad you're finding this so amusing." If she hadn't been the one living the embarrassing nightmare, she would probably be laughing, too.

"I am. I'm sorry, but I really am," Alison said between laughs. "You seriously couldn't get off of him?"

"Not at first, no, but I managed, obviously, and figured it was okay. I'd take what little was left of my dignity, which was precious little, mind you," Camellia took a drink of wine, "and do the elevator ride of shame back to my own room, get ready for my flight and head home. I'd never have to face Eric again."

"I'm guessing that didn't happen," Alison surmised. She topped off her wine and nodded in the direction of Camellia's glass. "More?"

"No, thanks." She set her hand over it to keep Alison from pouring her more wine. "I still have to drive," Camellia said, "and no, things didn't quite happen the way I figured, because would you believe of all the daily flights from Miami to Dallas, Eric would happen to be booked on the same one as me?"

"Oh, no," Alison said.

"Oh, yes."

"Did you run into him at the airport or something?"

"Nope. He didn't have his own car, so he needed a ride to the airport."

"And you gave him one?"

"I did, because I'm nice," Camellia said. "Okay, except maybe ignoring him the entire drive wasn't so nice, but what was I supposed to say?"

"Very awkward," Alison said.

"Right? It gets worse, though. The flight's not full, so he manages to charm the gate agent into changing his seat so he can sit next to me. Can you believe that?"

"He wanted to sit next to you? Ah, Cam, is this story turning romantic now?"

"No." Camellia glared at her friend. Naturally, Alison would see romance in everything. "Not unless you count offering to help me with the seat belt extender as romantic." She grimaced at the memory. "I mean, what does Eric know about seat belt extenders? And hello, fat girl here. I've been dealing with those hideous contraptions pretty much my entire adult life."

She drained the last of her wine, wishing she didn't have to drive home, because she'd love another glass. "I seriously wanted to die. Like, if the airplane door could have opened up and sucked me out, that would probably be a better fate that having to spend the two-and-a-half-hour flight sitting next to him."

"Oh, come on. It couldn't have been that bad, once the initial awkwardness passed," Alison said. "Unless, of course, when you landed, his girlfriend was there to meet him. Oh my God." Her eyes grew wide. "That didn't happen, did it? Please tell me that didn't happen."

"No. He says he doesn't have a girlfriend. I'm not sure I believe him, but whatever. He also says he's not going to forget about me. I'm also not sure I believe that." She let out a sigh. "He's got my number now, and I have his. Not that I have any intention of calling him," Camellia said, "but he sounded pretty persistent."

"He did? Wow, that's so sweet. I thought you said this story wasn't romantic."

"It's not. Wipe the dopey expression of your face. This isn't one of those Hallmark movies you love to watch," Camellia said. "He was probably just trying to be nice. I don't expect to ever hear from again." Which was just as well because she might be too mortified to see him.

"I bet you're wrong."

"Whatever." Camellia took her empty glass to Alison's sink. "Thanks for the wine, but I should head home."

"Okay, but are you free for lunch tomorrow?" Alison asked. "Gina's back in town, and I'm sure she'd love to hear about your wild and passionate night with Eric Grady."

"I'm sure she would, too." Camellia groaned. "She didn't date him in high school, did she? Please tell me she didn't date him."

"No way. Gina only had eyes for Corey," Alison assured her. "I'll call her."

"Fine. Anna's helping at the shop tomorrow, so I can meet you for lunch," she said. "Text me the when and where."

"Will do," Alison said. "And let me know if Eric calls tonight."

Chapter Eight

Eric didn't call that night, and by the time Camellia met Alison and Gina for lunch at a local deli they all enjoyed, she was resigned to thinking he wouldn't. Which was fine, she told herself. She never expected him to in the first place, and besides, she didn't want to hear from him again, anyway.

Except she did, which infuriated the hell out of her.

Naturally, Gina found the story as amusing as Alison had, which infuriated Camellia even more.

"I need some less obnoxious friends," she muttered to herself as she bit into her pastrami and Swiss sandwich on a garlic toasted pumpernickel roll. With Russian dressing, it was sure to exceed her calorie count for the day but eating here was a guilty pleasure Camellia allowed herself from time to time.

"Come on," Gina said. "We're laughing because we care about you."

"If you say so." Camellia studied her potato salad, which she'd opted for instead of fries. She always liked the potato salad, but it didn't stop her from gazing longingly at the sweet potato fries on Gina's plate. "It doesn't matter, anyway, because he's not going to call."

"He'll call. Give him time."

Camellia glared at Alison as she sipped Diet Coke through a straw. "New subject. Gina, how was your trip?"

Gina was an interior designer with her own popular TV show, and she had just returned from filming in Atlanta, where was redoing a home for a basketball star and his girlfriend, and Camellia always enjoyed hearing about her glamorous life. Before Gina could launch into a story, though, Camellia's phone rang.

She glanced at the name on the display. Eric. "Crap. It's him."

"So, answer it," Alison urged.

"I can't. I don't know what to say."

Gina rolled her eyes. "'Hello' is usually a fairly safe bet."

When Camellia made no move to pick up her phone, Gina reached for it. "Oh, for gosh sake, it's not that difficult." She swiped at the screen. "Eric, hi. It's Gina Masters."

To Camellia's horror, Gina put the call on speaker so they could all hear Eric's voice. "Gina? What are you doing answering Cami's phone?"

"You call her Cami?" Gina let out an amused chuckle. "Oh, Eric, do tell."

"Give me that!" Camellia grabbed her phone out of Gina's hand and quickly turned it off speaker before putting it to her ear. "Eric? It's just me now. Sorry about that. I have obnoxious friends who think they're comedians." She sent Gina a dagger.

He laughed. "That's okay. I was calling to see if you were busy, but I guess that answers my question." He sounded disappointed. "I was hoping to see you."

He was? "I'm having lunch with Gina and Alison right now," she said. "The aforementioned obnoxious friends. I'll be at my shop later, though, if you want to come by?"

"I'd love to," Eric said. "I've got some errands to do, but I'll look for you there later. Is it difficult to find?"

"Not at all. Just put in 'Flower Therapy' in Flower Mound and your GPS should bring it up. I'm right next to a bank."

"Perfect. I'll see you later, Cami. Enjoy your lunch."

Camellia set the phone down and looked at friends. "That was Eric. He's coming to the shop later."

"Yes!" Alison pumped a fist in the air.

"See, that wasn't so hard, was it?" Gina asked.

"No, but let's tap the brakes a little bit here," Camellia said. "For all I know, he's coming to tell me he has syphilis."

Alison expression turned horrified. "Oh my God, Camellia, stop it." And then, "You did practice safe sex, I hope."

"Yes," she snapped, sending daggers Alison's way. "What kind of idiot do you take me for?"

"You're not idiot, and I'm sure that's not why he's calling," Gina said. "Give it a chance. Eric's always been a good guy."

"Thanks, Gina," Camellia said. "That's reassuring. You knew him better than I did in school."

"Yeah. I can't wait to tell Corey. He's been afraid Brit might try to sink her claws into Eric," Gina said, referring her boyfriend's ex-wife.

"Say what?" Alison frowned. "I thought Brit was dating that cop?"

"I think that may be history, but I'm not sure, since I've been out of town for three weeks." Gina waved a hand. "I don't want to talk about Brit's love life. Let me tell you about my client and his girlfriend. What a total beotch..."

AFTER TALKING TO CAMELLIA, Eric put the name of her shop into the search bar on his phone. She was right. It popped up right away and wouldn't be difficult to locate with the help of GPS.

The listing showed that the shop was open until five that evening, which left Eric trying to figure out how best to plan his visit. Since he knew Camellia was having lunch with her friends, he didn't want to be too early, and there might be advantages to showing up later in in the day, like closer to closing time. If she didn't have other plans, maybe Camellia would want to spend the evening with him?

Ugh. When did he get to be so pathetic? It had never been difficult to get a woman to spend time with her. From the beginning, though, back to the first night in Miami, Eric sensed Camellia was different.

He walked Lizzie and answered emails, trying to pass enough time before driving down to Flower Mound. When he spotted a supermarket a few blocks away from Camellia's shop, he got an idea. He pulled into the lot and used his phone to find the number for Alison's clinic. Eric didn't know if she'd be available, but it was worth a shot.

"This is Alison Reisetter."

"Hi, Alison. It's Eric Grady, from Westfield."

"Yes, hello, Eric," she said. "This is a surprise, although maybe it shouldn't be. I assume this has something to do with Camellia?"

There was no sense beating around the proverbial bush. Obviously, what happened in Miami hadn't stayed in Miami, and Alison was fully aware of what happened between him and her best friend. Eric wasn't sure if that was a good thing or not. "Yes," he said. "I'm about to go see her, and I was wondering if she likes flowers?"

Laughter came over the line. "She owns a flower shop, Eric. I think it's safe to assume she likes flowers."

Sheesh. He was an idiot. "Okay, great, do you happen to know what kind? I want to get her some. Or maybe that's a terrible idea and I should go with chocolates, instead?"

"Not chocolates. She's always trying to lose weight."

"Right. I knew that." Yep. Idiot. "Flowers, then?"

"Yes, I think that's your safest best," Alison said. "Irises. She loves irises. And her favorite color is yellow."

"Got it. Thanks, Alison. I appreciate the help." It was good to have an ally, if in fact she was one.

"You're welcome. I'm pulling for you," she said, "but Eric?"

"What?"

"If you hurt my best friend, I might have to kill you."

Okay. Sort of ally. "I don't intend to, but message received, loud and clear. Thanks again. I have to go buy yellow irises now." Eric ended the call and headed inside the store.

Fifteen minutes later, armed with a bouquet of yellow irises from the supermarket down the street, Eric parked in front a nice brick building with yellow awnings and a bright yellow sign which read 'Flower Therapy' in pink letters. It struck Eric as a happy place, which was fitting given the name and the owner.

Since yellow was so dominant in the shop's signage, he had to assume Alison was right about it being Camellia's favorite color and she hadn't, in fact, steered him in a bad direction.

Clutching the flowers in one hand, Eric locked his car and headed toward the front shop's front door. It chimed as he opened it, and Eric found himself surrounded by flowers. More of them than he ever thought possible, and he'd just come back from a whole conference on flowers. In addition to the flowers, though, there was a section of home décor, as well as lawn ornaments. Cute. Colorful. Happy. Like Camellia herself.

An attractive young blonde stood behind the counter, and she greeted Eric as he approached. "Hi. Can I help you with something?" She wore a nametag which read 'Anna' and there was something oddly familiar about her, even if Eric was certain he'd never seen her before.

"Yes. I'm looking for Camellia," he said. "Is she here?" She'd assured him she would be, and Eric didn't want to believe she'd stand him up.

"Yep. She's in her office in the back. Just a minute." Anna stepped out from behind the counter to a hallway and called out, "Hey, Mom. Someone's here to see you."

Mom? Eric found himself dumbstruck, but it explained why Anna's face was familiar. She was the spitting image of Camellia, who had just emerged from her office. She wore white jeans and a short-sleeve yellow shirt, and with her blonde hair pulled back in a ponytail through a matching yellow cap sporting the name of the shop in pink letters, she looked pretty and happy, and younger than her years.

"Oh, hi Eric," she said. "I see you've met my daughter, Anna. Anna, this is Eric Grady. We went to high school together."

"A long time ago," Eric said. "Your mom's aged better than me."

"I doubt that," Camellia countered, chuckling.

"I brought you these." Eric handed her the flower bouquet. "From the grocery store down the street, which I realize is probably completely lame, but hey... it's the thought that counts, right?"

"That's right." Camellia accepted them from him with a smile. "Thanks. They do a decent job there, and I don't get flowers very often," she said. "Which is too bad, because I obviously love them."

She handed the bouquet to Anna. "Would you mind putting these in water while Eric and I talk?"

"Sure thing, Mom," Anna said, and Eric tried to read the look that passed between them. It was too quick, though.

"Thanks." Camellia turned to Eric. "Let's go back to my office. I'm sure you have questions."

"A few, yeah."

Chapter Nine

Camellia left Anna to attend to the flowers—the bouquet really was quite nice—and led Eric back to her office. There was a small circular table in the corner, which she used when talking to clients, and she gestured for him to have a seat. Once he did, she sat down in the other chair.

"The look on your face says it all." This wasn't how she intended him to find out about Anna, but then again, she hadn't anticipated he would ever find out, because Camellia didn't expect to see Eric again at all. And then he showed up at her shop with a bouquet of irises. She loved irises. And they were yellow—always a win.

"You have a daughter." Eric raked a hand through his hair, causing it to spike a little on the top. He really was impossibly handsome.

"I do, indeed."

"You're not married, are you?" His gaze landed on her left hand, though it wouldn't have offered him any clues. She seldom wore jewelry, other than her smart watch, because rings and bracelets got in the way of her work. "Please tell me you're not married."

"No, I'm not married." Camellia choked out a laugh. "Dodged one there."

"Whew." Eric exhaled sharply, his relief evident. "I'm guilty of many things, but I've never slept with a married woman before, and I don't intend to start now," he said. "Divorced, then?"

She shook her head. "No. Never married. Anna's father, if you can call him that, has never really been part of her life, or mine." The less said about Philip Sloane the better.

"That's his loss, then," Eric said, and Camellia smiled.

"I tend to agree. Anna's a great kid."

"I'm sure she is, but I was referring to you."

"There you go saying nice things again and sounding sincere while you do it." Camellia stood and walked over to the small refrigerator beside her desk and pulled out two bottles of water. She handed one to Eric as she returned to the table.

"Thanks," he said. "Hey, you're not using your crutches."

"No. Around my shop, and at home, I usually don't need to," she said. "I know the layout, and things are arranged so that if I do have a balance issue, I can grab on to something and steady myself."

"That's terrific." Eric uncapped the bottle of water and took a drink. "How old is Anna?"

"Twenty-two," Camellia said. "I got pregnant right out of college, which forced me to make some hard decisions, especially when I realized that if I had the baby, I'd be raising her alone, but that's the choice I made, and I've never regretted it or second-guessed it."

She took a drink of water. "Anna studies graphic design at TCU and works with me here part-time, and she has a wonderful, supportive boyfriend who treats her like the princess she is, so at least she's not following in her mother's footsteps of regrettable choices with the opposite sex."

When Eric raised an eyebrow, she laughed and quickly added, "Present company excluded, of course."

"That's better," Eric said. "At least give me a chance to treat you well before you write me off."

"I'm trying. I mean, you're here." For all his talk the day before, this was still unexpected. She'd heard talk before.

"Yes, I am, and I intend for that to continue. I meant what I said yesterday." Eric took another drink, set the bottle down. "You must be very proud of Anna."

"She's the best thing I've done with my life, by far." Camellia waved her hand around the room. "This, my shop, is the second best," she said. "If nothing else, I've raised a good kid and built a good business." Most days, it was a fulfilling life.

There was a knock on the door to her office. "Come in."

Anna opened the door and stuck her head in. "Hey, I'm sorry to interrupt, but I've got to head out for my workshop now. Do you want me to deliver the birthday bouquet for Ms. Lewis on my way out?"

"Thanks, but you don't have to," Camellia told her. "I can take it when I leave. It's not due until six, and it's right on the way home. Just get to your workshop."

"Will do," Anna said. "I've got class all day tomorrow, so I won't be in."

"Yep. I know," Camellia said. "I've got my book club in the evening, so I guess I'll see you Wednesday. Bye, kiddo."

"Bye, Mom. Nice to meet you, Eric."

"You, too, Anna."

"And be nice to my mom, okay?" she added before leaving.

"I guess she put me on notice," Eric said after the outer door chimed, signaling Anna had left the shop.

"Yeah. For two decades, it's always been just the two of us, so we look out for each other," Camellia said, standing. "Would you like me to show you around the shop? I mean, I know flowers aren't really your thing, but—"

"They weren't before this past weekend, that's true, but I seem to be taking an interest in them now," Eric said. "I'd love to see your shop."

ERIC MIGHT NOT KNOW flowers, but he at least thought he could recognize an organized, well-run, and successful business when he saw one, and this was it. He particularly loved the branding and color scheme, which was present throughout the shop. "You mentioned Anna is a graphic design major. Did she do your branding?"

"Yes. Do you like it?"

"I do. It's very eye-catching."

"I told her I wanted yellow and pink, because they're my favorite colors," Camellia said. "Bright and happy, that's what I envisioned, and she just ran with it."

Her face beamed with pride when she spoke of her daughter, making her appear even prettier. "Bright and happy," Eric repeated. "It suits you, Cami." And yellow was a great color on her.

"I have to lock up and make this delivery, but if you want to tag behind and follow me to my house, we can talk some more," she said, "and I can probably even come up with something for dinner."

Eric smiled. "That sounds good. I'd love to see your house, and it's not like I have anything better to do tonight." Lizzie would be fine for a couple more hours—he could always have Tess check on her—and he'd deleted his so-called little black book from his phone.

"So, you're saying I'm your last resort? Now who's wounding who with their words?" Camellia quipped as she shut off the lights. "Can you hold this for a second?" She handed Eric the bouquet, which he readily accepted.

"That was intended as more of a referendum on my pathetic life than a slight against you," Eric assured her.

"I know it was. I was teasing." She armed the alarm and locked the door behind her before reaching for the bouquet again.

"I've got it." He carried it to her car and set it inside.

"Thanks. The delivery will be quick, and I'm just a few blocks away."

She was right, and ten minutes later he followed her into a cul-de-sac and parked next to her in the driveway of an attractive single-story house with a lush green yard. At least in Eric's estimation, it had the best landscaping of any of the houses. He wasn't surprised.

"Welcome to my humble abode," Camellia said as she led him up the front walk and unlocked the door.

"It's lovely."

She laughed. "The inside is a bit messy, but in my defense, I was out of town for the weekend."

"I can relate and promise not to judge." Inside, the foyer ked to an expansive living room with large windows looking out to a beautiful backyard.

"There's nothing here top secret, so feel free to wander a bit while I go change clothes," Camellia said before disappearing down a long hallway.

Even if she said to wander, Eric didn't feel comfortable snooping, so he stayed in the living room. To his left was a dining room and open-concept kitchen. The wall opposite the couch featured a large TV and built-in bookshelves. Since he knew Camellia was a reader, he headed that way, deciding maybe he would snoop a bit, after all. A person's book collection could reveal a lot about them.

He didn't get that far, instead finding himself distracted by a framed picture on the fireplace mantel. It was of a pretty young woman, obviously Anna, in a graduation cap and gown, standing next to... was that Camellia?

"I see you've discovered that infamous photo."

Eric turned around. She'd changed into pink leggings and an over-sized T-shirt, and her blonde hair now fell loosely to her shoulders in soft waves. "Yes. I assume it was Anna's high school graduation."

"Yes, and yours truly, topping the scales at about 345."

"I almost didn't recognize you."

"That's good. I don't recognize myself most days," she said. "Also good."

Eric didn't know what to say. "Have you always..." He started, then stopped.

"Been fat?" Camellia supplied.

"I was going to say, 'struggled with your weight,' but that doesn't sound much better, and now I'm kind of feeling like a jerk."

"You're fine, and the answer is kind of a yes and no," she said. "I've never been thin. If you remember me from high school, I was always on the fluffy side. That continued through college. It was after I had Anna that things kind of got out of control. I was a single mom, and child support was sporadic at best, so I found myself working two jobs, going from one to the other and picking up drive through fast food in between. Not the healthiest lifestyle, and my self-esteem wasn't the best at the time, either. I don't even think I realized how bad things had gotten, though, until I looked at myself in the mirror the morning that picture was taken, and I hated what I saw."

"Oh, Cami." Eric could see the tears welling in her eyes, and he moved toward her, wanting to comfort her, but she held up a hand.

"Please, let me get this out, and then we won't speak of this again." She wiped at her eyes. "That was four years ago, and around the same time as my diagnosis. We talked about this a little in Florida. But, anyway, long story short... I got the message, loud and clear, that things needed to change, and with the support of my daughter and my best friend, they did," Camellia said.

"I quit the dead-end job I hated, and that kept me confined to a desk. I taught myself floristry. I joined a gym and started focusing on my health. I cashed in my 401k, leased a building for my shop, and bought myself this house. I'm still a work in progress, but I like myself, and my life, a whole better these days, and next spring, when Anna graduates from college, we'll take another picture." She paused. "My goal is to be on the right side of 200 by then, but that's still a little ways off."

"You look amazing, and I'm not just paying lip service." Unlike the picture on the mantel, her face was no longer bloated. Instead, her facial features were clear and defined, and her body featured curves in all the right places. Eric sensed that if he kissed her right now—and oh, how he wanted to—they'd probably end up in her bed in a matter of minutes.

Camellia must have sensed it, too, because she took a step away from him. "There's shade out back. Why don't we get something to drink and sit outside?" she suggested. "I have iced tea or lemonade."

"Whichever you prefer," he said.

"I've got wine, too, but after what happened in Miami, we might want to lay off that."

Eric raised an eyebrow. "What happened to no regrets?"

"I don't regret anything," Camellia said, "but if you're determined to embrace the other night as something other than wine-fueled sex, then it seems prudent to at least figure out how we feel about each other when we're sober, don't you think?"

"If you insist." Eric followed her into the kitchen, admiring the view from behind as she walked.

Chapter Ten

Camellia made her way to the kitchen to get the drinks, cognizant of Eric's eyes on her the entire time. This type of attention from men—good, healthy attention—was unusual, but she had to admit it was flattering. "Since you said you had no preference, we're having sweet tea," she declared. "Because southern girl here."

"That's fine." Eric didn't sound like he cared.

"I'm not even looking at you and I can tell that you're checking out my ass," Camellia said as she opened the refrigerator, "which makes me think hot pink spandex on one of its considerable size was a bad idea."

"On the contrary, I think it was a great idea," Eric said. "I'm trying to figure out why I've never dated a curvy woman before."

"Oh, that's easy." She opened a cupboard and got out two of her favorite tea glasses and filled them with ice from the dispenser on the refrigerator. "You're a very fit, handsome man, with a certain degree of celebrity, at least locally," she said. "Therefore, society expects you to date only beautiful women, and our society objectifies women. The thin ones are beautiful. The rest of us, well..." She focused on pouring tea, then adding a slice of lemon and a fresh mint leaf to each glass.

"Our society can be stupid."

Camellia let out a hiccup of laughter as she turned around. "No kidding? Honestly, I've lost count of how many times I've heard 'Well, she has a pretty face, if only she'd lose the weight.' Like, gee, thanks for telling me I have the potential to be attractive, if only I were thin." She shook her head. "If I had a dollar for each time, I'd own a vacation home in St. Lucia by now." She held out the two glasses of tea. "Do you mind carrying these, and I'll lead the way to the patio?"

"Perfect. That means I can check out your ass some more."

"Feel free, but if you think it's too big, kindly keep your opinion to yourself."

"Trust me, Cami, that's not what I'm thinking at all."

That was exactly the problem. It was difficult to discern exactly what he was thinking. He said all the right things, and he'd certainly done all the right things in Miami, but now that they were home, what were his intentions?

She'd given him the out. The chance to walk away. One wild, drunken night in Florida. Yet here he was, at her house, helping her carry sweet tea to her patio. And he'd brought her irises, even if they had come from the grocery store two blocks from her shop.

Camellia opened the double doors which led to her backyard, which was her favorite part of the house. With eastern exposure, it was shady and comfortable in the evening, the perfect place to sit and have a drink and watch the sunset.

"This is nice," Eric said, setting their drinks on the patio table.

"It's usually very pleasant this time of day."

"You have your own garden, I see."

"Yes. It's part of my healthy eating routine," she said.

"What do you grow?"

"Lettuce, tomatoes, carrots and snow peas."

"Really? That's cool." He sounded genuinely impressed.

"I enjoy it. It gets me outside, enjoying the fresh air, and like I said, I definitely eat healthier these days." She sat down in one of her patio chairs. "Feel free to walk around a bit if you want," Camellia told Eric. "I've been on my feet most of the day, so I want to sit."

"Then I'll sit with you." He took the seat opposite her and picked up his glass of tea, taking a drink. "Mmm. This is good."

"I'm glad you like it." She raised her own glass to her lips, enjoying the subtle sweetness. "I've perfected the recipe over the years," Camellia explained. "Some people make it too sweet for my taste."

"It's delicious." Eric swirled his glass, studying it. "Is this a mint leaf in here?"

"It is." Camellia chuckled. "I didn't think you were paying any attention when I poured it. This confirms it."

"No. Guilty." He smiled that sexy smile of his. "I must've been too busy checking out your ass."

"Must've been, yes." Why did he have to be so darn charming? They sat in silence for a few minutes, occasionally sipping sweet tea while not so subtly studying each other from opposite sides of table.

"If you don't have other plans, I can fix up a salad for dinner with stuff from my garden," Camellia said, breaking the silence. "I have some sliced ham to put in it, and I can boil a couple of eggs."

"That sounds great, and I'd love to stay," Eric said. "Though I'm a little offended you might think I have other plans. I already told you I didn't. I also brought you flowers. I'm sitting here in your garden, drinking southern-style sweet tea and admiring your ass." He paused. "All right, since your ass is sitting in a chair right now, I am unfortunately not currently able to admire it. I can, however, admire the rest of you, and I'm doing that with no thought as to what you could change. This isn't just me killing time before a date with someone else, Cami. Every damn word I said on that plane yesterday was the truth. I like you, okay? A lot."

Camellia waited a beat before replying, letting his words sink in. If Alison or Gina were here, they would undoubtedly chastise her for letting her insecurities boil to the surface yet again. "Okay." She sucked in a breath. "I like you, too. Also a lot."

Eric smiled. "Then now we're getting somewhere," he said. "All I'm asking for is a chance to prove I'm serious. Can you give me that?"

"And you're not here to tell me you have syphilis?" she asked, immediately regretting the question when Eric choked as he swallowed.

"What?"

"That came out poorly. It was a joke with Alison and Gina at lunch," Camellia said, and explained told him about the conversation with her friends.

"Hopefully with context, you're less offended," she concluded.

"Yes. And no, that is not why I'm here. I'm disease free. I can provide documentation if needed."

"That's good to know. I can't get pregnant, so when—I mean if—we…" Camellia stopped talking as the heat rose to her cheeks. What on her possessed her to go down this road?

"When we sleep together again?" Eric's face broke out in a grin. "Well, now we're getting somewhere."

"I said 'if.'"

"You said 'when' first."

"Freudian slip," she countered.

"Yeah, and you know what they about those…"

"You're enjoying this, aren't you?" Judging from the smirk on his face, he was enjoying it quite a lot.

"I've enjoyed every moment I've spent with you so far," Eric said. "And yes, I am now very much enjoying looking forward to that when."

ERIC ALREADY KNEW CAMELLIA was different from any other woman he'd ever dated, and he had some work to do to win her over and convince her he was for real and that was before she leveled him with her blunt—and brutally honest—assessment of why he'd never dated anyone who looked like her before. Hell, the contacts he'd just deleted from his phone were proof that she was right. He could handle it, though. He thrived on a good challenge, and he'd beaten long odds before.

"Would you like more tea?" she asked, with a nod in the direction of his near empty glass. "And I can fix that salad now, too, if you're ready?"

"Sure." He stood, picking up the glasses. "Let me get these."

"Thanks. I'd rather not stumble on my own patio trying get two of my favorite tea glasses into the house."

"I don't know why, but I love that you have favorite tea glasses." He admired the etched gold design on the blue glass. "These are pretty."

"They're imported from Morocco. A housewarming gift from Alison when I moved into this house," Camellia said. "So, there is some sentimental value there."

"Nice," Eric said. "Do they come in other colors?"

"Red and green. Two of each."

They were talking about tea glasses. And Eric liked it. Yeah, Camellia was different, all right.

Back in the kitchen, she refilled their tea glasses and busied herself removing sealed plastic containers from the refrigerator, which he assumed contained the ingredients for the salad.

"Do you need any help?" Eric asked.

He saw her hesitate, and figured she'd say no, but then she surprised him. "There's a big mixing bowl in the cabinet over the sink. Would you mind grabbing it?"

"Not at all." He located the bowl, set it in front of her on the counter, stealing a look into the containers she was busy opening. Lettuce. Tomatoes. Snow peas. All fresh from her garden. "This looks delicious."

"I picked all this from the garden when I got home yesterday afternoon," Camellia said. "I hope you like it. I had a big lunch, hence the lighter dinner."

"It's fine." He just wanted to spend time with her.

She got a few eggs from the refrigerator and placed them in a pot with water and set it on the stove. "These will take about ten minutes. Sorry I don't have any ready, but I wasn't planning on entertaining tonight," Camellia explained.

"Don't apologize. I can wait," Eric said. "Are you sure there's nothing else I can do to help?"

Camellia shook her head. "I've got it, thanks. Just have a seat at the island," she said, and then added, "You can check out my ass some more."

Eric grinned. "In that case, carry on." He pulled out one of the stools at her granite-topped center island and sat down. He leaned forward, resting his elbows on the counter. "View's great from here."

"You amuse me, Eric," she said with a laugh.

"I'm glad." His eyes scanned the room. "I like your kitchen."

"Me, too." Camellia turned around to face him. "Gina redid it for me last year."

"She did? Wow."

"Yeah, prior to that, it was screaming mid-1980s. I don't think it had been updated since the house was built," she said. "I loved the house but hated that kitchen. Now, I love the kitchen, too, which is good because I do a fair amount of cooking these days."

Camellia returned to prepping the salad, and Eric returned to his new favorite pastime of watching her. He hadn't seen her use her crutches the entire time he's been there, and she moved with ease around her kitchen. He found it quite remarkable because she had seemed so reliant on them at the conference, but perhaps it was simply a matter of not trusting herself in unfamiliar surroundings and around a lot of people.

"What kind of dressing do you like? I've got Ranch, Caesar, or Balsamic vinaigrette."

"Ranch."

"Ranch it is." Camellia set the dressing on the island, followed by two large salads. "I thought we'd just eat in here, if that's okay?" she asked, pulling out the other stool. "Rather than carry everything outside."

"Works for me." Eric reached for the bottle of Ranch, generously dousing it on his salad. He noticed Camellia, by contrast, used only a small amount of the vinaigrette on hers.

He picked up his fork, ready to dive into the salad, when he remembered Lizzie. "Crap." He reached into his pocket, pulling out his phone.

"Is something wrong?" Camellia frowned.

"No," he assured her. "Just something I forgot to do." He typed in a quick text to Tess and returned the phone to his pocket. "All good now."

Then he noticed the look on Camellia's face.

"Canceling plans you just remembered you had?"

THE WORDS WERE NO SOONER out when Camellia wanted to take them back, and she silently cursed her insecurities. "Sorry. It's none of my business."

"Actually, it is," Eric said. "I'm sitting here with you. I've professed my interest in you. You have every right to know if I'm being disingenuous and sneaking around." He pulled the phone from his pocket again, entered his passcode and handed it to her. "Go ahead. Read the text."

Camellia wasn't sure she wanted to, or if she should, but her curiosity got the better of her and she looked at the screen. The recipient was named Tess, ostensibly a woman, and the text read:

I'm having dinner at a friend's house. Can you please go check on Lizzie for me? Make sure she has water and doesn't need to go out?

The reply read simply:

Of course. Have fun.

Casual. Friendly. But not at all flirty or sexual. Camellia handed the phone back, feeling like an idiot. "I think I can safely assume Lizzie is a dog."

"Yep. Lizzie is a two-year-old yellow lab, and my heart belongs only to her." Eric scrolled through his phone, then held it up, showing Camellia a picture.

"She's beautiful," Camellia said. "Who's Tess?" She was careful to keep any accusatory tone from her voice.

"Tess is my fifty-seven-year-old widowed next-door neighbor," he said. "No, I haven't slept with her."

"I didn't ask."

"No, you didn't. Just putting it out there," Eric said. "Her dog, Chloe, is Lizzie's mama, so Tess is always up for checking in on her when I'm not home, and dog-sitting when I travel."

"You're lucky to have a neighbor you can count on, especially since you travel s much."

He nodded. "I know. Tess is great. Do you like dogs, Cami?"

"Is it a deal-breaker if I say no?"

"Not at all," he said quickly, but he did appear disappointed.

"Good." She laughed. "I love dogs, by the way."

"You were testing me?"

"Maybe a little," she admitted. "When I say I love them, though, it's with a caveat. Big ones make me a little uneasy, because I worry they might jump on me, and with my balance issues..." She felt it had to be said, because Eric's beloved Lizzie was obviously a larger dog.

"Understood. When you meet Lizzie, I'll keep her back until I know you're comfortable and make sure she doesn't jump," he assured her. "She's a really good dog."

"I'm sure she is." Camellia smiled. "I notice you said 'when' I meet her, not 'if.'"

"Good catch," he replied, and took a bite of his salad. "This is delicious, though it might be better with a glass of wine."

She recognized his tone as teasing, and chuckled. "I agree, but I know what happens when you drink too much wine."

"Yeah, and the other night in Miami, I seem to recall you liked it a lot."

"Touché." Camellia would give him that one.

"I understand what you're doing, or trying to do," Eric said, "with this whole thing about making sure that wasn't just wine effects, but Cami?"

"Hmm?"

"I'm stone-cold sober right now, and I still really like you," he said, "and I also think you're sexy as hell. Just, you know, pointing that out."

She could feel the heat rise to her cheeks. Yes, he got to her, all right. "So noted."

Eric grinned. "Also, you're even sexier when you blush," he said, "and I love that I can make you blush."

Camellia bit her lower lip. She was determined that he wouldn't end up in her bed that night, but with each sexy smile and flirtatious comment, her resolve weakened. He was smooth, real smooth, and it didn't help that no man had made her feel this way in a very long time, if ever. "I'm sure you do."

He took a bite of salad and washed it down with tea before asking, nonchalant as ever, "What are you reading for your book club?"

"You're interested in my book club?" She regarded him with surprise.

"I'm interested in you, and I know your book club is important to you," Eric said. "That makes me interested in it, yes. Also, you're probably the most intelligent woman I've dated in a long time."

Camellia raised an eyebrow. "There are so many ways I could respond to that, but I think I'll just say thanks. I think?"

"You were right about me, and the women I've dated," he said. "I have tended to go for the types that exemplify society's stupid definition of beautiful. Young, skinny and shallow. Why? Because they make me feel good about myself, like I'm still some sort of celebrity or something. Which is pretty stupid, since I haven't been much good at anything since my time at Florida State, and even then, it was mostly my receivers that made me look a lot better than I was." He paused, taking a drink. "Is there any more tea?"

"In my house, there's always more tea." Camellia stood and went to the refrigerator to get it, grateful for the distraction, because how was she supposed to respond to what he said? She hadn't intended to make Eric feel bad about himself at the expense of feeling better about herself.

"The book is about a baseball player, during spring training in Arizona," she said, pouring them each more tea, even though neither glass had been empty.

"And a women's book club is reading this?"

"Yes. It wasn't my choice, but it's interesting," Camellia said.

"Are you a baseball fan?" Eric asked.

"Not really, but Anna's boyfriend plays for TCU, so I know a little about it."

"I know a few pro ball players," he said, "from events that I do."

"It's a good book, but I still have forty pages to finish tonight to see how it ends," she said. Even reading on the flight home yesterday, she hadn't been able to get it done. Probably because she was too distracted thinking about Eric.

"Then I should probably be going soon," he said, but made no move to get up. "What time does your club meet tomorrow?"

"Six to eight," Camellia said. "We have appetizers, wine and talk about the book."

"It sounds like fun."

"I enjoy it a lot."

"So, you're home by what? 8:30, 8:45?"

"Closer to 8:45, with traffic," she said. There were times she missed the smaller towns in Alabama, even if she'd now called the Dallas area home for more than half of her life. "Why?"

"I thought I might call you, if that's okay," Eric said. "I'd like to hear more about the book."

"Sure. That's fine." She doubted he cared about the book.

"Great. I look forward to it." He stood now, carrying his plate to the sink. "I need to get home to check on Lizzie and leave you to your reading," Eric said. "I enjoyed this a lot, though. The salad, the tea, the conversation. Thank you."

"You're welcome. I enjoyed it, too." More than she cared to admit.

"Thank you. I'll talk to you tomorrow," Eric said, brushing his lips across hers. "Happy reading, Cami."

Chapter Eleven

Eric waited, not so patiently, until 8:45 to call, trying to give Camellia plenty of time to get home, but she still sounded out of breath and distracted when she answered.

"Hey. I'm going to put you on speaker for a minute if that's okay?"

Like he had a choice? "Is this a bad time? You're not still in the car, are you?"

"No, it's fine. I just walked into the house. I was just about to change clothes."

"Is this book club formal, or something?" Eric asked. He'd already been mildly curious about it, mainly because everything about Camellia intrigued him. Now, he was more intrigued. "Do you dress in fancy gowns and sip tea?"

The delightful sound of her laugher reverberated across the line, with an additional echo because she had her phone on speaker. "Hardly. We drank Pinot Grigio and ate hummus with pita chips and mini quiches from Costco," she said. "But I left straight from work, so I'm ready to get out of those clothes."

"Does that mean you're naked right now?" Eric asked hopefully. "Because I can be there in fifteen minutes."

More laughter. Good. Eric loved her sense of humor and appreciated that she got his, rather than taking offense. "You flatter me, but not tonight. It's been a long day," Camellia said. The echo over the phone lined faded, and Eric assumed he was no longer on speaker. "Besides, I'm not naked. I just put my PJs on. They're white, with yellow daisies on them, and I'm fairly certain I look like a beached whale in them."

"I'm fairly certain I wouldn't agree, and that I'd find them sexy," Eric countered, "but okay. I'll put the car keys down. Reluctantly."

"Thanks. You do flatter and amuse me, Eric," she said, "and I like it."

"Then I'm doing something right." He'd been joking, mostly, about going to her house, but if Camellia had been at all receptive to the idea, he would've have gotten in the car. It wasn't as if he had anything else going on, other than watching a bad movie on Netflix.

Check that. Since he wasn't going anywhere, Eric kicked off his shows and leaned back in his recliner and found a baseball game on TV. He had a seventy-two-inch screen, an IPA from his favorite local brewery, and Lizzie perched beside his chair. It wasn't a bad life, and far better than where he'd been a dozen years ago, when he was at his lowest of lows, but it wasn't wholly satisfying, either.

Camellia could change that, if only she gave him the chance.

"Are you going to tell me about the book you read for your club?" he asked.

"If you care, and you really want me too," she said.

"I am legitimately interested," Eric said. "Partly because the club is obviously important to you, and I want to learn as much about you as possible, and partly because I'm an avid reader myself." He could never talk about books with any of the other women he dated—slept with—and already loved that she was different. "I know that probably surprises you, given my dumb jock image in high school, but it's the truth. It's enjoyable and relaxing to escape into a fictional world, you know? Especially when your own real world isn't much fun at all."

"Believe me, I know that all too well," Camellia said. "That's why I love books, all of them. As someone who has dealt with depression, and spent plenty a night hating myself, it can be a great escape to read a steamy romance set in the Regency area. Or, heck, even a non-fiction piece about the Roman empire. I mean, at least it was different from my own life, with a job I hated, my ballooning weight and the useless ex who never paid child support." There was a lull of silence before she spoke again. "You didn't call to talk about that, though."

"I called to hear your voice. We can talk about anything you want," Eric said. He doubted that was her ex, though, or her struggle with her weight, so he moved to change the subject. "Have you actually read about the Roman empire or were you only watching *Gladiator* for Russell Crowe?"

"That, Eric, is none of your business," Camellia said. "But if you insist on knowing, I have both read about the era and ogled Russell Crowe."

He laughed. "At least you're honest."

"Always."

"Are you going to tell me about the book now?"

"I could, but I'm not sure you want to hear about this particular book."

"Why?" Eric asked. "You said it was about a baseball player." He glanced at the TV screen. "I enjoy baseball. I'm watching a game right now. I'd probably like the book."

"I'm less sure about that," Camellia said. "It wasn't just about one baseball player, but rather multiple ones, during the trials and tribulations of spring training. One became addicted to gambling. Another was addicted to pain meds."

"Oh. Well." Eric's hand clenched as he reached for his beer. "That sounds very uplifting. Or not."

OR... NOT. SHE'D BEEN enjoying their playful, flirtatious banter, but then the real world had to intrude. It was kind of like reading. A person could escape into a different world, usually one a lot more enjoyable than the one they lived in, but it couldn't last forever.

This...whatever it was... that was happening between she and Eric was amazing, but Camellia didn't expect it to last. For as long as it did, though, she intended to enjoy every minute of it. Just like she didn't want the great Regency love stories she read to end, Camellia didn't want this to end, either.

"I did warn you that you probably didn't want to hear about it," she reminded him. "The last thing I want to do is remind you of past demons. I've had enough trouble vanquishing my own."

"See, maybe that's why we work so well together," Eric said. "We've both had to slay all these dragons and demons, and yet we've come out on the other side."

Has she, though? It didn't always feel like that. "I'm not sure I've slayed them," Camellia said. "There's always a risk they'll rise again." Her MS, her weight, her depression. All things she was mostly in control of right now, but they could still rear their ugly head again at any moment.

"Did you ever play pro football again, after you were released by Miami?" she asked.

There was a brief pause before Eric said, "I love that you asked that. It tells so much about you. Most of the women I meet only want to hear about the good times. The Texas high school championship with Westfield. The National Championship with Florida State. My rookie year with the Dolphins, before the knee blew out and the wheels fell off. You, though, you ask about the rest," he said. "Even when the whole sordid tale is available on the internet if you care to look."

"I know that, but I haven't cared to look," Camellia said. She'd been tempted a couple times, but decided she'd rather hear it from Eric himself, when and if he was ready. "It would feel too much like a breach of trust. I'd rather you tell me."

"In that case, yes, I did," Eric said. "The Bills took me on a few years later. I insisted I was clean and sober, and they gave me a chance as a reclamation project." A bitter laugh followed. "It's a quarterback driven league, and they were desperate at the time. They had to be, to think I could save them, when I was drowning myself."

"You weren't clean, then?"

"I was... mostly," Eric said. "Or I believed I was. But you've heard what they say about relapse being part of recovery?"

"I'm familiar with it, yes."

"It proved to be all too true in my case," he continued. "I was doing fine. Not great, but fine. I was starting for Buffalo, playing decent. We won some games, and there was talk I was back. Then I got injured again. It was only a high ankle sprain. Hardly as catastrophic as my knee injury. It scared me, though. More than I cared to admit." There was silence before Eric spoke again.

"I stole a few Vicodin from the team doc, washed them down with whiskey, and got behind the wheel of my car," he said. "And spun out on black ice, wrapping it around a guardrail."

Camellia sucked in a breath. "Oh, Eric."

"That night marked the official end of my football career, but I figure I got pretty lucky, because it could've been the end of my life."

"I'm glad it wasn't."

"You and me both," he said. "After that, I went off the grid for a few years, trying to get my shit together, before attempting another comeback as a broadcaster."

"That didn't work out, either?"

"Nope. See, you're good at this game," he said. "Turns out people want to see Super Bowl MVPs and present and future Hall of Famers broadcast the games, not washed-up former addicts."

"C'mon, Eric," Camellia said. "Don't call yourself that. It's defeatist talk."

"Maybe so, but you call yourself fat. Is it any different?"

"Perhaps not, but I am fat."

"You keep saying that, and I still think you're beautiful," Eric said. "And I am still a former addict."

"That doesn't bother me if it doesn't bother you."

"It doesn't, not anymore," he said. "It's only part of who I am."

"Just like fat and disabled is only part of who I am," Camellia said. "I love that you want to know the other part."

"I do. Very much," Eric said. "Thanks for listening tonight."

"My pleasure. I enjoy talking to you." And the more she did, the more Camellia realized they had in common.

"Likewise."

"It's getting late, though, and I have to open the shop in the morning," she said. "Maybe we can do something this weekend, though?" There she was, initiating something. And it wasn't completely uncomfortable. Actually, it felt kind of good.

"I'd love to, but I have a guy thing Friday night."

"A guy thing?" Camellia chuckled. "Whatever that means."

"It's no different from your book club, really. It's just guys. We drink beer. Play pool. That kind of thing."

"Sounds fascinating," she said. "What about Saturday, then?" Hopefully, she didn't sound too desperate."

"I'm flying to Boston Saturday night for a speaking engagement on Sunday," Eric said. "It's a one-day thing, but they'll pay me well."

"That's good then." Camellia tried to hide her disappointment.

"How late is your store open on Saturday?" Eric asked.

"Only 'til three. Why?"

"Maybe I can swing by your house on the way to the airport? See your beautiful face and have a some of your famous sweet tea?" he suggested. "If you have some"

"I always have sweet tea, Eric, and you're more than welcome to come over to my house for a glass anytime."

"Great. It's a date, then. I'll see you Saturday."

Chapter Twelve

She hadn't been home from the shop more than ten minutes before Eric got there, which left her no time to straighten the place up or change clothes. Camellia did have sweet tea, though, so there was that.

"I missed you this week," he said, as he sat perched at her kitchen island while she prepared the tea—because true southern sweet tea involved more than simply pouring it from a pitcher into a glass.

Camellia had to admit she missed him, too, even if she was only ready to admit it to herself. "How was your 'guy thing' last night?" she asked instead.

"It was fine. Jack is a buddy of mine from my short-lived time at CBS. It was his birthday, so we got together to shoot some pool and have a couple beers," Eric said. "Nothing too exciting."

"No naked women, then?"

"Nope, and had they been there, they couldn't hold a candle to you, anyway."

"Oh, right. Whatever." He might be a master of flattery, but that one was a tough sell. Camellia held out a glass. "Here's your tea."

"Thanks." He accepted the glass from her and took one sip before setting the glass down. "It's good, as always, but I think there's something else I want more right now."

"What's th—" The last word was swallowed in a kiss, and the second Eric's lips were on hers, her body reacted, and Camellia knew.

Miami wasn't a fluke. It wasn't the wine. There was so much more happening here than drinking too much and fulfilling a high school fantasy twenty-seven years too late.

She might not be the most experienced when it came to carnal pleasure, but nor was she innocent. Camellia knew what she liked, knew what felt good, and she knew when a man was turned on—and Eric was turned on.

"Jesus, Cami, the things you do to me," he said, his breath hot against her neck. "I missed you. I just wanted to stop and say hi on my way to the airport. Really, my intentions were good." He shifted his position, and she could feel his erection press against her.

"Well, you know what they say about the road to hell." At that moment, she was more than willing to go down it. "What time is your flight?"

"Not for a couple hours, and I'm not checking luggage."

"It's twenty minutes to the airport from here." Emboldened, she put her hand to Eric's crotch, feeling his arousal through the fabric of his pants. "Think you can make it?"

He let out a guttural sound. "I'm willing to try."

"I was hoping you'd say that." If he missed his flight, Camellia intended to make sure it was worth it for them both. "Not here, though. I'm not having sex on my kitchen island."

"You think Gina would be offended?"

The very thought made Camellia laugh. "Gina would offer hearty congrats and give me a high five," she said. "I was thinking about my back and my legs." It was so unromantic, though, to have to pause and give mind to her physical challenges. "Can we just go to my bedroom?"

"I'd like that very much. Please lead the way."

She did, closing the door behind them. "Sorry. I didn't have time to make the bed this morning." Her mother, a slightly obsessed bed-maker, would be mortified.

"It's okay. We're going to mess it up more anyway."

"True. Feel free to hurry. We can always go for slow and sensual next time," Camellia said, pulling her shirt over her head. There was no point in being self-conscious now He'd seen her naked. He knew her curves and her pillowy thighs, and everything about his physical reaction to her told her he liked it.

"Good thinking. I like that," Eric said, shedding his own clothes.

God, he was beautiful, with his long, lean and hard body a total contrast to hers. Yet somehow, they fit together. When the doorbell rang just as he moved between her legs, ready to enter her, Camellia cursed under her breath.

"Are you expecting someone?" Eric asked, pausing above her.

You. Inside me. "No. I'm not answering it." Except the next sound she heard was her daughter's voice.

"Mom? Are you here? Your car's out front. I tried calling your phone..."

"Shit. It's Anna." Camellia sat up.

"She has a key to your house?"

"Yes, Eric, my daughter has a key to my house." Was the door even locked? She didn't remember. Either way, in another minute or so, Anna would be at the bedroom door. Camellia needed clothes. Fast.

"I'm in the bedroom." Stark naked, with an equally naked man. "I'll be right out."

"Take my shirt," Eric said, handing it to her.

"Thanks." Camellia pulled it on, and since he was tall and she was short, it mostly covered her bottom. Getting it buttoned over her ample chest was another matter. This would be good.

"Anna, I wasn't expecting you." She was careful to block any view into the bedroom as she opened the door and closed it behind her.

"Yeah, the washer at my complex is broken. I was hoping to toss a load in here. What are you doing in bed this early? Are you sick or some..." Anna's voice trailed off as she apparently connected the all the dots. "Oh."

Messy hair, flushed face, clutching a man's shirt closed over her boobs. This was not a scene Camellia ever intended to share with her daughter. "I'm fine, but this isn't a good time."

"Yeah, I see that now. Is that Eric's car out front?"

"Yes." There was little point in denying it.

"Hello, awkward," Anna said. "I'll just show myself out."

"Okay. If you, um, want to put the laundry in..."

"No, Mom. The laundry will wait. I am now leaving."

Camellia found herself torn between wanting Anna to get out of there as quickly as possible and wanting to somehow salvage something from this mortifying moment. "We're still on for breakfast, right?"

"Sure," Anna said. "Same as usual. I'll see you then."

Camellia watched her leave before going back into the bedroom. "Sorry about that."

Eric sat on the edge of the bed. "Don't be. I'm fine." He turned, searching her face. "Are you?"

The concern in his voice touched her. "I will be. I realize the mood's probably gone now..."

"Actually, the mood is fine," Eric said, with a glance downward. "I think almost getting caught turned me on even more, if that's possible."

"In that case, let's finish what we started," Camellia said, dropping his shirt to the floor. She'd already died of embarrassment. Might as well make the most of it.

DELAYED TWO HOURS. He'd risked a speeding ticket racing to DFW—it would totally have been worth it—only to discover that he had two hours to kill before his flight to Boston. Eric planted himself at the bar across from his gate, ordered an IPA from one of the local breweries, and cast his eyes on the TV above the bar, which was tuned to a college football game.

He expected it might be Texas or Oklahoma. Maybe TCU or Baylor. No. Arkansas was playing Auburn. Camellia's alma mater.

Was the universe trying to tell him something?

Even though she insisted everything was fine when he left her house, Eric was less sure. He didn't like that feeling of uncertainty. Also, he already missed her. After forty-five minutes. Good grief.

He fished his phone from his pocket, found her name in his contacts—he wished the screen showed her actual photo and not an avatar—and tapped the screen to call her.

"Hey, are you at the airport? I hope you didn't miss your flight."

"No. It's delayed," Eric said. "Two hours. Rain in Boston, or something like that."

"Ugh. I'm sorry."

"Me too. I should've checked the status on my phone before I left." If he'd known about the delay, he could have stayed at her house longer. Eric was pretty sure they could've found a way to pass the time. "So, now I wait."

"What are you doing?"

"Having a beer and watching college football," he said. "Your alma mater is playing."

"Really? What channel?"

He told her. "They're losing right now, but they made me think of you," he said. "Then again, practically everything does these days."

"I doubt that, but thanks," she said. "Okay. Found the game. Oh, I miss that place."

"Why did you move back to Texas after college?" Eric asked. "You never told me." He just knew she missed Alabama.

"Because I was pregnant, alone, scared, and I needed my Mama," Camellia said. "It's fine. I've grown to love Texas, and I've built a good life here."

There was a pause as Auburn gave up a sack and the quarterback fumbled, giving Arkansas the ball inside the twenty. "Oh, have mercy. That play was hot garbage. If I'm going to watch this, I think I need wine."

"Oh, so now you're going to drink wine."

Camellia laughed. He could listen to that laugh all day. "Well, yes. I already ended up in bed with you again, didn't I?"

"Much to my very great pleasure, you did," Eric said. "Are we still good, though?"

"Why wouldn't we be? The sex was plenty good, at least from my end."

"It was spectacular from mine." Eric didn't want to think about it too much, though, because he might end up with a problem that would be hard to conceal. "What about Anna? I hope I didn't get you in trouble with her."

"Get me in trouble with her?" Camellia repeated, laughing. "First off, I'm the parent here. Second, it takes two to tango, Eric, and I was a more than willing participant on that dance floor," she said. "I'll own my own actions. Yes, it was embarrassing. When I meet Anna for breakfast tomorrow—like I do every Sunday morning—I'm sure it will be awkward at first. For both of us. I didn't date much when she was growing up, so this is new for her. She's a good kid, though, and we have a great relationship. We'll be fine."

"Okay. That makes me feel better."

"You really were worried, weren't you?" Camellia asked.

"Yes. Like I keep saying... I like you. A lot. And I'm trying very hard not to screw up what could be a wonderful thing." He screwed up practically everything else, but if there was anything he wanted to get right, it was this, because his life was already so much better with her in it.

"You should stop being so hard on yourself, because you're doing just fine."

MEETING FOR BREAKFAST on Sunday morning had been their tradition ever since Anna graduated and moved out on her own. It was something they both enjoyed, and Camellia hoped it would continue. Even with Anna working part-time at the shop now, she still treasured the time with her daughter.

This time, though, when she walked into the restaurant and joined Anna at their usual corner booth, Camellia had no idea what to expect. It didn't take long to find out, though.

They'd no sooner ordered—Anna's customary blueberry short stack and Camellia's biscuits and gravy—when Anna said, "I wasn't sure if you'd come alone or bring your new boyfriend."

So, that was the way it was going to be. "Have I ever not come alone? This is our time."

"If you say so."

"For whatever it's worth, Eric isn't even in town," Camellia said. "He had to fly to Boston for work last night. He just stopped by my house on his way to the airport. He lives up in Lewisville."

"How convenient for both of you." Anna's voice was laced with sarcasm. "You get your quickie, and he can even bypass the tollway."

"Anna Sloane Harris!" Camellia reached for her coffee, almost drinking it all in a single gulp. She was in no way prepared to deal with her daughter's hostility without lots of caffeine.

To her credit, Anna held her hands up in an apparent show of surrender. "I always know I've crossed a line when you hit me with the asshole's name, too." Anna had always hated that she had her father's last name as a middle name, because she was steadfast in her desire to have absolutely nothing to do with Philip Sloane. Camellia didn't blame her, and it seemed they all three felt the same way.

"If this is how you want to do this, then it seems pertinent to remind you that I am forty-five years old. I own a very successful business, and I live alone in a house in which I am the only person named on the mortgage. I have earned the right to invite anyone I want to into said house," Camellia said. "And yes, into my bed, too, if I so desire."

"Apparently you desired to yesterday afternoon."

Camellia was relieved when their food arrived at that precise moment, and that her coffee cup was mercifully refilled. It gave her the opportunity to regroup and maybe get the conversation on to a better track. Besides, biscuits and gravy helped everything, even if these weren't as good as the ones she got in Alabama.

"Yes, I did. Come on, cut me a little slack here. It's been a while." Surely, Anna would concede that point.

"That's for sure, and if I wasn't too busy being mortified, there's a part of me that would probably want to give you a fist bump and say 'Go, Mom.'"

That was better, and Camellia managed a half-smile. "If it helps, it was equally mortifying for me," she said. "But since when do you use your key to let yourself into my house when you see there's another car in the driveway? Is that not a clue that maybe I have company?" One thing was for sure—she doubted Anna would do it again.

"Since never, but like I said, I tried to call. I got worried when you didn't answer," Anna said. "I mean, you could've been in danger. There could've been a serial killer in your house who chloroformed you when you got home from work and slit your throat."

Camellia almost choked on a biscuit. "Have mercy, child. Your imagination is too much."

"What?" Anna was indignant. "It happens."

"Maybe in those awful horror moves you like to watch, but I think it's pretty uncommon in suburban Dallas," Camellia said. "In fact, I'm not aware of a single serial killer on the loose in my subdivision. I can check the neighborhood app, though, in case I missed an update."

That elicited a laugh from Anna. "Okay, I may have overreacted a little," she said. "I'm glad you were having hot sex rather than having your throat slit, Mom."

"Um, thank you. I think?"

"I'm mostly happy for you," Anna continued. "Eric seems nice enough, and he is kind of cute, for an old guy. I don't want to see you get hurt, though."

"I'd rather avoid it myself," Camellia said, "but if that happens, I guess it's a risk I'm willing to take. Because right now, in this moment, I'm pretty damn happy, okay? Can you give me that much?"

After a few seconds, Anna nodded. "Yes, but if he does hurt you, I'm going to have Gage beat him up. And I do mean that, Mom."

"Then let's hope it never comes to that, because I don't want your boyfriend ruining his baseball career defending my honor." Camellia speared a biscuit with her fork. "Now that we have that settled, what are you up to the rest of the day?"

"I have a design project to work on, but it can wait a bit," Anna said. "Why?"

"I thought maybe we could go to NorthPark Center and do a little shopping?" Camellia suggested. "Fall weather will be here soon and everything I have from last year is a size too big." It felt good to be able to say that.

"In that case, let's go." Anna grinned. "I'm always up for a little retail therapy with my favorite mom, and we can find you some sexy clothes to wear for your new boyfriend."

Chapter Thirteen

After fussing in front of the mirror for way too long, Camellia settled on wearing a new dress she bought on her shopping trip with Anna the week before. It was a shirred midi dress in a soft coral color, and when she'd tried it on, she'd been surprised at both how well it fit, and how nice it looked, considering it was a size smaller than she'd worn the year before.

It was more of a summer-style dress, but fall weather hadn't made it to Texas yet, and no one knew when it would. The color looked good with her blonde hair, and Camellia even did a half twirl in front of the mirror, smiling at her reflection.

Not bad. Not bad at all.

Especially considering that a few years before, she mostly hated her appearance.

She still wasn't to her goal of being below 200 pounds before Anna's college graduation, but the progress was noticeable, and she felt good, too. Having a sexy guy interested in her didn't hurt, either.

Yeah. That was worth a second twirl.

Camellia grabbed a light-weight shawl to wear over the dress, just in case it was cold in the restaurant. She didn't know where they were going—Eric insisted on surprising her—but she figured the dress and shawl would be appropriate regardless of the location.

It was dressy enough for fine dining, and she wouldn't be too over-dressed if the restaurant was more on the casual side.

All in all, a win. There was still the matter of the crutches, though.

She didn't want to take them. She didn't want to be reliant on them, and besides, she'd felt good lately, without any muscle stiffness or balance issues.

That was in her usual surroundings, though. Her store and her house, where she was familiar with the layout. Camellia had never been to Eric's house before and had no idea what she might find. Did he have a sloped driveway or lots of stairs? And what about his big dog?

Even though Eric promised to keep Lizzie from jumping on her, there was still a risk. And then there was the restaurant, too. Best to be on the safe side and take the crutches.

Eric's house was a modern two-story that, at first glass, didn't appear much larger than her own house. Camellia hadn't been sure what to expect, given Eric's storied past. Sure, he appeared to have built a successful career with his speaking jobs, but he hadn't played pro football in probably fifteen years. She wasn't expecting a multi-million-dollar mansion, and if she'd seen one, Camellia probably would've been intimidated.

She could handle this.

Eric came outside as she pulled into his driveway—thankfully, not sloped—greeting her first with a wave and a smile, and then a kiss on the cheek as she exited the car. "You look beautiful," he said, stepping back to study her. His smile showed he approved. "Did you have any trouble finding it?"

"No. GPS is a wonderful thing," Camellia said. "I'm excited to see your house." The idea of the stairs intimidated her a little, but maybe she wouldn't have to deal with them much.

"Then let me give you the tour," Eric said, leading her to the front door. "Lizzie is out back. I'll introduce you whenever you're ready, but no pressure."

"Thanks." They stepped into the foyer, which led to the kitchen, which wasn't large, but appeared functional.

"I know, the kitchen's not much, but I don't cook all that much, either," Eric said with a shrug. "I have steaks marinating, though, which I'll put on the grill."

"Steaks? I thought we were going out tonight." For the first time, she noticed Eric was dressed in jeans and a T-shirt. Certainly not something he'd wear to a nice restaurant.

"That was the original plan, yeah, but I changed my mind," he said. "I thought we'd hang out at Casa Grady instead. Grill the steaks and some vegetables and have wine. I hope that's okay?"

"Sure. It sounds great," Camellia said, forcing a smile to her face. She'd looked forward to going out, but she'd adapt. The company was what mattered.

HER SMILE, WHICH NORMALLY lit up her whole face, now seemed forced, which brought Eric back to the Miami airport, when Camellia's normally sunshiny mood turned tense.

"Are you sure?" He probably should have called her earlier to discuss the change in plans, but he hadn't expected it to be a big deal. Now Eric wondered if that was a miscalculation on his part. "If you really have your heart set on going out to dinner, I can put the steaks back in the fridge and change clothes, and we will."

"On short notice, on a Friday night, without a reservation?" Camellia shook her head. "We've both know how hard that is," she said. "This is fine."

"Okay." He hoped she was telling the truth and he hadn't messed something up. "Next time we'll go out," he told her. "Anywhere you want to."

"That sounds great," she said. "C'mon, let me see your house."

"It's nothing too fancy," Eric said. "There are two bedrooms upstairs, but the master's down here, so you won't have to worry about climbing stairs if you don't want to."

Camellia let out a laugh. "You sound awfully confident you'll get me into that bedroom."

"Yeah, maybe a little." He tried for his most charming smile. "I did say we were having wine, you know," he teased. He also recalled it hadn't taken that the last time.

"Anyway, the grand tour of Casa Grady..." He took her around the downstairs of his house, showing her the kitchen, living room, and a small study. It didn't escape Eric's notice that Camellia used her crutches here, in the unfamiliar space.

"You weren't kidding when you said you like to read," she observed, noticing the wall-to-wall bookshelves in the study.

"Nope. I didn't say it only to impress you."

"I never thought you did," she said, "but I didn't expect a collection like this, either." Camellia studied the rows of books. "You even have all the classics.

"I'm glad I could surprise you," Eric said. "I'm honestly a little jealous of your book club," he told her. "Being able to get together with good friends and drink wine while you talk about books. Are you sure I can't come and crash it sometime? Do they allow significant others to tag along?"

Camellia laughed. "That's like me asking if I can crash your billiards and beer nights with your guy friends."

"I don't mind if you do," Eric said, "but it's not a regular thing like your book club."

"Sorry, but the book club is ladies only," Camellia said. And then, "Am I officially your significant other now? Is that what we're calling this?"

"Well, you're becoming pretty significant to me," he said. "I guess it's up to you to decide how significant I am to you." Eric hoped he had at least achieved the level of somewhat significant. "Would you like to see the aforementioned bedroom?"

She cocked her head to the side. "You're not subtle, are you?"

"Nope. Subtlety is vastly overrated." Eric led her to the bedroom, where they remained in the doorway. For now.

"I even made the bed this morning," he said, and she laughed.

"Are you trying to show me up?"

"Maybe a little," Eric said. "We'll get back to this later—yes, I'm confident—but let me show you the backyard and introduce you to Lizzie. I promise I'll keep her from jumping up on you." She usually didn't, anyway, but he sure didn't want this to be the time she did.

"Thanks. I appreciate that," Camellia said. "I do want to meet her."

The double doors off the living room went to the back patio, and Eric opened them. Right away, Lizzie came running over to him. "Hey, girl," he said, kneeling and putting a hand on her back. "Daddy has someone he wants you to meet. This is my friend Cami, and she's very special, so you have to be good, okay? That means no barking or jumping."

He stood up, keeping in front of Camellia, just in case Lizzie disobeyed him, which was rare. No, she stayed still, looking up at them.

"Hi there, Lizzie. It's nice to meet you," Camellia said. "I've heard a lot about you."

"She's heard a lot about you, too," Eric said. "We talk a lot."

Camellia laughed. "Does she answer you much?"

"Nope, but I know she hears me." Eric gestured to the outdoor loveseat. "Go ahead and have a seat, and I'll get us some wine."

"That sounds great."

He waited until she sat down before going inside and retrieving a bottle of wine and two glasses. Naturally, Lizzie followed him, but when they got back outside, Eric noticed the dog went to the side of the loveseat where Camellia sat, settling by her feet. "I think she likes you," he observed.

"It's mutual." Camellia reached out to pet the dog while Eric sat down.

He opened the wine, pouring them each a glass. "This is a Chardonnay from a local winery," he said, handing her the glass. "It came highly recommended, so I hope you like it."

Camellia took a drink and nodded her approval. "It's delicious, thank you."

"You're welcome." Eric settled next to her, putting an arm around her shoulder. "I can start the grill in a bit, but I thought it would be nice to sit out here a bit. Talk, relax, and no interruptions like we'd have at a restaurant." That had been his thinking, and he hoped she understood.

"This is perfect, Eric," Camellia said, and it sounded like she meant it.

CAMELLIA SET THE ALARM on her phone mainly as a precaution, fully expecting to be awake before it went off. She almost always was. This time, though, it roused her from a deep slumber. "Sorry," she muttered, reaching to silence it as Eric stirred beside her.

"Is that an 'I have to jump out of bed right this minute' sort of alarm?" he asked. "Or more of a 'I should think about maybe getting out of bed, but I still have a little time' alarm?"

"The latter." Camellia chuckled at his characterization. "The next one will go off in half an hour." With that one, she'd have to move fast in order to make it home before she had to open the shop.

"Good. We still have some time, then," Eric said.

"Mm hmm. Do you have something in mind?"

"Maybe." He moved closer, pressing his hardness against her. "See, I have this little problem."

"Oh, that." Camellia rolled over to face him, lifting her leg over his so he could slip inside her. "That's not a problem for me if it's not a problem for you."

It turned out lazy, wake-up sex could be very satisfying, but work beckoned. Camellia hurried back to her house to shower and dress for work, making a mental note to take clothes with her the next time she planned on staying at Eric's. Okay, last night she necessarily planned to, but she should have recognized it was the likely outcome.

She arrived at the shop five minutes before she was supposed to open it and was just getting out of her car when Anna pulled into the lot, parking next to her. Camellia waited for her. "How's my favorite daughter this fine Saturday morning?"

"Good," Anna said. "Are you just getting here?"

"Yeah." Most of the time, Camellia was there a half an hour before opening, and Anna knew it. "I overslept this morning," she said, unlocking the door. "And then traffic." Camellia flipped on the lights and disarmed the alarm.

"Traffic? You live five minutes from here," Anna pointed out needlessly. "Unless you happened to be coming from another suburb. Like, say, Lewisville?"

"Yes, fine. I stayed over at Eric's. I'm allowed to do that." She busied herself making sure all the window blinds were raised to the same level.

"I didn't say you weren't." Anna went to the front counter and booted up the computer. "So, where did you guys go last night?" she asked. "And more importantly, what did you wear?"

"The coral dress. I've decided I love it," Camellia said. Eric had, too. "We ended up staying in, though, and Eric grilled steaks." The steaks were great, and so were the marinated veggies, and they'd sat out on the patio, first watching the sun go down and then enjoying a soft breeze as they finished the bottle of wine.

"Oh. Lovely."

"Yes." There was an edge to Anna's tone that Camellia didn't think she liked. "It was a lovely evening." Probably better than it would have been if they'd gone out to a restaurant, and certainly more private.

"Yeah. I'm sure it was." There was the tone again, only more obvious this time, and now Camellia was certain she didn't like it.

"What is that supposed to mean?"

"Huh? Nothing," Anna said.

"Really? Because it sure sounded like something."

Anna let out a sigh. "Okay, fine, if you insist. I just find it interesting that here you were, all excited about going out to a nice restaurant and wearing your new clothes, and instead you end up staying in and, well..." Anna's voice trailed off, letting the unspoken words hang in the air. "That's your prerogative, of course, but next time maybe ask yourself whether you're actually having a relationship here, or simply fulfilling a high school fantasy."

Whoa! Camellia was certain her jaw dropped, and she found herself struggling to form a response.

Before she could, the phone rang. Saved by the bell.

"I'll get that," Anna said, grabbing the handset. "Good morning, Flower Therapy. Anna speaking." After a pause, she continued. "Yep, she's right here, Mrs. Jennings. Hold on just a minute." She put the call on hold.

"It's Barb Jennings from the church, about today's order."

"Like clockwork," Camellia said, chuckling. Barb could be demanding, but the church was one of the shop's most lucrative contracts, so Camellia wanted to keep her happy. "I'll take it in my office," she told Anna. "If you can make sure the lights are on in all the display cases."

"Got it."

"Thanks. And Anna?"

"Yes, Mom?"

"Do me a favor and worry about your own relationship and let me handle mine."

Chapter Fourteen

Anna didn't mean any harm. Camellia was sure of that. But once the seed of doubt was planted, it was difficult to keep it from growing. It was like an insidious weed. Weeds didn't need the careful attention and love that flower beds and gardens did. Weeds simply festered.

So did insecurities, especially ones that had been festering for most of Camellia's life.

On the way back from a visit to her doctor, Camellia decided to swing by Alison's office. Maybe her friend would be able to see her, and she could get this nagging feeling of doubt off her chest. She hoped so, because it was dragging her down, and Camellia hoped to avoid going down that dark road again, especially when she'd just gotten a good report from her doctor.

Cassidy, Alison's long-time receptionist, recognized her from her days as an official client—even if it had been a couple years—and sent Camellia back to Alison's office once she received the okay.

"You look fabulous, by the way," Cassidy added.

"Thanks." Camellia wished she felt that way, and most of the time, she did. Other times, the old demons returned.

"This is a surprise," Alison said. "I assumed you were working today. I hope nothing's wrong."

"Anna's covering the shop. I had an appointment with my neurologist, who's in the area," Camellia said. "I thought I'd swing by. I hope you don't mind. The check-up went well. Dr. Harlowe thinks my MS might be entering remission, and—"

"And stop babbling, Camellia," Alison interjected. "I'm thrilled if the MS is in remission, but I've known you since we were fifteen, and I know when something is wrong. You showing up at my office is a sure sign something is."

"Fine." Camellia huffed out a breath. "I need to talk. Feel free to bill my insurance if you need to."

"Oh, good grief. You know I won't do that," Alison said. "I'm ethically prohibited from accepting payment if I don't think you would benefit from therapeutic services."

"Well, don't be so sure that I won't," Camellia muttered under her breath.

"Nope, not going there." Alison shook her head. "Let's just talk, as friends. Forget I'm behind a desk in my office. You're one of my closest friends. And please don't take the 'one of' as a slight, because Gina is your friend, too. It's not a competition."

"I know. I wasn't going to take it as one."

"Good. So, what's wrong?" Alison asked. "If you just got a good report from your doctor, you should be beaming."

"Oh, but I am." Camellia forced a smile to her face. "See. This is me. Beaming."

"Okay, stop it. What's really going on here? Does this have something to do with Eric?" Alison let out a sigh. "Of course, it does. Am I right?"

"Yes." There was little point in denying it. "I think I have to end things with him." She didn't want to, but the alternative might be even more painful.

"Are you kidding?" Alison asked. "You've been so happy ever since you guys connected in Miami. Like walking on air for the past month. I thought things were going great." She frowned. "Did you have a fight?"

"What? No." The idea struck Camellia as ludicrous. "We never fight. Most of the time, when we're together, all we do is laugh."

"Yeah, that sounds awful, all right."

Camellia waved that off. "It's not awful. It's... wonderful," she said. "When we're not laughing, we're talking about books or movies. Did you know he loved Invisible Man, way back from Miller's AP Lit class?"

"I didn't, no," Alison said.

"He did, and now he's saying he wants to join my book club, which I'm thinking Sienna might not be keen on, but—"

"Camellia, stop!"

"What?"

"What is your problem? Why would you want to break things off when Eric when it's going so well, and you're obviously happy?" Alison asked, and then she frowned. "Did he cheat on you? Because if he did, I can have Gina kill him for you."

Camellia choked out a laugh. "Why Gina?" She frowned. "You're not willing to kill for me?"

"I didn't say that. I totally would," Alison insisted, "but Gina has more money and connections, so she's more likely to get away with it. Plus, I have the kids to think about," she said. "Ellis and Mason are probably old enough to deal with it, but I like to think Laken would miss me if I went to prison."

"He for sure would, and you're right about Gina," Camellia said. "Either way, it doesn't matter. Eric didn't cheat on me." She believed him when he said that wasn't the way he rolled. Besides, the sex they were having was incredible. "That's not the problem."

"Then what is?" Alison asked. "Talk to me, Camellia, and I don't care how long it takes, because more than anything, I want to see my friend happy, and up until about twenty minutes ago, I thought you were."

"I am. I just... please don't think I'm crazy."

"I'm a mental health counselor. I assure you, that's the last thing I would ever think."

ERIC DIDN'T CONSIDER himself particularly good at planning surprises, but then again, he didn't get much opportunity to do it. He lived alone with his dog and dated shallow women who looked good on his arm because, hey, they took very little effort. He was good-looking, drove an expensive car, and had just enough local celebrity left that he was considered a catch, at least if they didn't dig too much into the archives on The Dish Zone. Or worse yet, the police blotter in Buffalo, New York.

These days, the celebrity gossip site liked to refer to Eric as a pathetic, over-grown man-child, and it wasn't too far from the truth. Or it hadn't been until about a month ago. Who would've believed one trip to Miami—Miami, of all places?—would change his life?

Well, as it turned out, Miami wasn't too bad to him.

He placed a couple of quick calls, making sure everything was in place, before calling Camellia. Eric hoped she wouldn't balk when she learned what he had planned. Maybe he should've discussed it with her beforehand, but then it wouldn't be much of a surprise, would it?

Ugh. Hopefully, he hadn't screwed this up.

"Hey, sexy," Camellia said when she answered.

"I thought that was my line," Eric protested. "You're the sexy one."

"And that is why it's so hard to quit you. You call me 'sexy.'"

"You are sexy," he said. "And why would you ever want to quit me?" Was she seriously considering it? No. It had to be just a figure of speech. "Are you at your shop?"

"No, but I'm heading there now," she said. "I had a doctor's appointment at Southwest Medical Center."

"Are you okay? Nothing's wrong, I hope?" No, Eric, don't let your mind go there.

"Nope. Everything's fine," Camellia said. "Actually, it's all good news. Maybe we can go out somewhere tonight? Like Monarch?" she suggested, referring to the upscale restaurant on the 49th floor of Santander Tower in downtown Dallas. "I've always wanted to go there."

Eric had never been there either and always vowed that if he ever did dine there, it would be with someone special. Well, what was he waiting for? "We'll go there sometime," he said, "but I have a little surprise for you today. How far are you from your shop because I was planning to meet you there."

"I'm about fifteen minutes away," Camellia said. "Anna's there, though."

"Then I'll beat you. I guess I can wait in the car 'til you get there."

"Why? I just told you, Anna's there."

"Yes, but I'm not sure your daughter wants to see me right now." Or rather it would be extremely awkward for Eric, considering how close they came to Anna walking in on him having sex with her mother.

Camellia laughed. "I promise, it's fine. That was weeks ago. We're all good now. And since she knows your car, I can promise there will not be a repeat interruption."

"That's good to know," Eric said. "Okay, I'm almost there. I'll be sociable and face your daughter, but please hurry, Cami."

"Right. Tell that to the traffic. I'm working on it."

He pulled into the lot and shut off the engine. Did he have to go in? Yeah, he promised he would. It still felt a little bit like facing a firing squad.

The door chimed, signaling his arrival, and Anna greeted him from the counter with a smile. "Hi, Eric. You don't mind if I call you that, do you?"

"Uh, no. It's my name." He looked around the shop, his eyes landing on a ceramic frog holding a flower umbrella. Cute. "I know your mom's not here, but she's on her way back."

"Yes. She had a doctor's appointment, but I guess you knew that."

"Yeah, that's what she said."

"She called me just now and said she was on her way," Anna said. "She told me to be nice to you."

Eric smiled. "That sounds like Cami." He wondered if her daughter would heed the advice.

"I can't believe you call her that. No one has ever called her that."

"Maybe that's why she likes it when I do," Eric said. It was a theory, anyway.

One Anna rolled her eyes at. "Whatever. I know you're sleeping with her."

"Yes." There was no point in denying the obvious. "We're both single, consenting adults."

"I'm aware of that."

"Good. About what happened a few weeks ago…"

Anna held up a hand to stop him. "Let's not go there, okay? It is what it is," she said. "I want to make sure we're clear on something here, though."

"What's that?"

"My mom really likes you. I'm not sure you're all that, but she seems to think you are, so that's cool with me," Anna said. "Mostly."

"Mostly?" Eric repeated, raising an eyebrow.

"Yes. What I mean is, you better not hurt her, because no one—and I do mean no one—deserves happiness more than my mom. So, you know, please don't turn out to be a douche canoe like every other guy she's ever dated, because if you do, just be aware that you and I are going to have real problems," Anna said. "Or rather you will, because I will send my boyfriend after you, and he's twenty-five years younger, so I'm pretty sure he can take you."

The door chimed again, and Anna turned in that direction. "Hi, Mom. Eric and I were just talking."

CAMELLIA COULDN'T TELL for sure what she'd just wandered in on. Anna had plastered a phony smile to her face, while Eric looked slightly constipated. All in all, it could probably be worse.

"Well, if it isn't my two favorite people." She walked over to Eric, giving him a kiss on the cheek, before asking Anna, "Did I miss anything exciting here?"

"Not really. It's been quiet."

"Yeah. It's that time of year." She shrugged. "Death season will be here soon enough."

"My God, Mom, you're so morbid." Anna turned to Eric. "I don't know if you've seen this macabre side of her, but she gets some sort of thrill about people dying, because she makes money off of it."

"It's not quite like that," Camellia protested. "And Eric knows, because he spent two days with a bunch of crazy florists at our conference."

"That's right. It was an eye-opening weekend," he said. "Not to mention life changing." His lips curled in a mischievous smile as he winked at her. "Right, Cami?"

That smile. Seriously. That smile made Camellia weak. Alison's advice was spot on. She shouldn't make an impulsive decision to end things without at least talking to Eric about her concerns. "Right," she said. "So, what beings you here? What's this surprise?"

"Can you leave town for a couple of days?" Eric asked. "I know it's spur of the moment and I probably should've said something before, but I wanted it to be a surprise."

"Leave town?" Was he serious? "What about the shop? I can't just lock the door and leave." Except she could, if she wanted to, because she owned the place. Self-employment had its perks.

"You did say it's the slow season," Eric pointed out. "We'd be back on Sunday, and you're closed then, anyway, so you're really only missing the rest of today, and tomorrow."

"He's right, Mom. And you close at three tomorrow, anyway," Anna reminded her. "It's not very long. If you're that concerned, though, I'll cover things. I'll stay the rest of today, and I'll open tomorrow morning. I've helped you with the order for the church enough times that I know can handle it myself," she said. "Plus, I can have Gage help, too, if I need it."

Camellia wasn't sure her daughter's baseball player boyfriend would be much help working in a flower shop., but she appreciated the gesture. "Are you sure? What about school?"

"I don't have class on Fridays anyway. That's why I'm here," Anna said. "I can handle this, Mom. The only thing that will be hard is if any custom orders come in, but all your designs are on your computer, right? I can replicate them. Plus, I can Face Time you of I need help, right?"

"I suppose." There likely wouldn't be any orders come in that needed that short of a turnaround time, anyway. "You're right. It'll probably be slow."

"Then you should totally do this. You deserve to get away for something other than a work trip."

Now Anna and Eric were co-conspirators? What was she supposed to make of that? Her daughter was right, though. Camellia hadn't taken any sort of vacation in years. What was the point, when there wasn't anyone to take it with? And really, nagging self-doubt aside, she'd have to be out of her mind to pass up this opportunity. "Well, when you put it like that..."

"Great." Eric grinned. "I'm glad that's settled. We should probably hurry. You'll need to pack some things."

Talk about a whirlwind morning, and it was barely ten o'clock. "Will you at least tell me where we're going?" Camellia asked Eric. "How will I know what to pack."

"Seasonal," Eric said. "Like, Texas seasonal." He started ushering her to the door. "We should go. We'll swing by your house so you can pack, and we'll leave your car there."

"Eric, this is crazy," Camellia protested. It was also rather fun and exciting.

"Go, Mom. You deserve this," Anna said, before turning to Eric. "Take good care of her and remember what I told you."

"Got it," Eric said. "You heard her, Cami. Let's go. We have a plane to catch."

So, they were flying, but apparently not leaving the state. Camellia wondered when the next clue would drop. "What was that all about at the end?" she asked as they walked to the parking lot. "What did Anna tell you? And I still think this is crazy."

"I know that, but I'm asking you to embrace the crazy. All will be revealed in due time."

Embrace the crazy? Whatever that meant.

Thirty-five minutes later, after a very quick stop at her house, where Camellia haphazardly threw clothes into a bag, they arrived at the airport. Instead of going to the commercial passenger terminal, though, Eric headed toward the parking area for private jets, and when he gave his name to a security officer, they were ushered through.

What on earth was going on?

"And there it is, ready and waiting," Eric said as he parked his car in a spot designated for private and charter passengers. "Wait until you see the inside of this thing."

Thing, as in the plane sitting on the tarmac, ready to whisk them away to God knows where.

"You have your own private plane?" Camellia stared at Eric in disbelief.

"Me?" Eric laughed. "No. Don't you read the gossip sites? I'm little more than a washed-up former addict trying to recapture his glory years. I do, however, have friends in high places."

Camellia wanted to correct his assessment of himself, but sound herself still rather in awe of the plane. "I suppose that's better than having them in low places."

"Oh, baby, I've got them there, too." Eric grinned and held out his hand to her to help her up the steps. "Are you coming?"

"You still haven't even told me where we're going," she pointed out.

"No, because it was intended to be a surprise," Eric said. "If you insist on knowing before you get on the plane, though... the flight plan has us landing in Brownsville. We'll rent a car there and drive to South Padre Island for a couple of nights."

"Padre?" Camellia blinked. "Why?"

"That part is going to have to remain a surprise," Eric said. "At least for now. A man must have some secrets. I promise it'll be worth it, though," he added with a wink. "And hey, private jet. You know, in case you want to rethink that mile high club thing."

Camellia rolled her eyes. "You're incorrigible," she said, taking his hand. "But okay, Padre it is." And that mile high club didn't sound like too bad an idea.

Chapter Fifteen

Her eyes darted around the beach, taking in the scene. It was a beautiful fall day, not too hot, and Camellia still couldn't believe she was here, or that she'd flown here aboard a private plane. Maybe she should've have taken that whole mile high club thing more seriously, because really, when she was likely to be on a private jet again?

She'd woken up that morning thinking it was time to end things with Eric, and now here they were, strolling along the beach at South Padre Island, his arm around her waist as they walked—sans crutches—with a cool breeze blowing through her hair.

"This is gorgeous," she said. "Although I still don't know why we're here."

"Do we have to have a reason?" Eris asked. "Other than I have a friend who decided to lend me the use of his plane, and I wanted to whisk you away for the weekend?"

"I suppose not." She should stop second guessing everything and simply embrace this for what it was—a walk along the beach with a sexy guy she'd been crushing on for almost thirty years. "I love the beach. I love water," Camellia said. "I think one of the hardest things about learning I had MS was the fear of losing my mobility and realizing I might never be able to run along a beach and experience the feeling of the sand between my toes as I ran."

Sand, and beaches, were uneven and prevented too many obstacles for people with balance issues.

"I'm sorry. I'm sure it's difficult," Eric said, "but you're here, and you can look at the water. You can still enjoy it."

Simply looking at it wasn't the same, though. Not even close. "I want to do it," Camellia said. "I'm going to do it. Right here. Now."

Eric blinked. "Do what?"

"Run along the beach, barefoot, and feel the sand between my toes." She bent down and slipped off her shoes—plain, ugly canvas slip-ons that she wore without socks—and handed them to Eric. "Will you hold these for a minute?"

"I guess, yeah, but are you sure you should do this?" His expression was one of concern.

"No, but I need to do it." She hoped Eric would understand that. Four years ago, she could barely walk more than a hundred feet without getting winded, and every joint in her body ached.

Now, Camellia took off running. She wasn't fast, but she was running, and it was liberating. Exhilarating. The breeze blew through her hair, and she exulted in it.

And then ... splat! She landed flat on her face.

Okay. Not graceful. Not even close. But as Camellia sat up, stretched her legs, moved her ankles and knees, she realized she was fine, and she burst out laughing.

"Cami! Oh my God, are you okay?" Eric came running over, falling to the ground beside her, still holding her shoes. "Did you hurt yourself?"

Her knight in shining armor, or so he appeared to be, but suddenly all her doubts from earlier in the day came flooding back, and Camellia started to cry. "I'm fine. Physically, anyway." She wiped at her eyes. Her pride was wounded, and her heart might be breaking, but she'd be able to walk away. Or at least limp. Slowly.

"Then why are you crying?"

"Because I don't think I can do this anymore." She had the right idea before. She needed to end things before they got further long. Before she fell further in love with him.

"Do what?"

"You. Me. Us." She shook her head. "I can't do this, Eric. It hurts too much."

"Okay, back the truck up. What are you talking about?" he asked, his expression blank. "I know I'm not the sharpest tool in the shed, but I'm legitimately confused here, because I thought things were great. I mean, we're at the beach. It's a beautiful day. What could be better than this?"

Not much, probably. That was the problem. "Nothing," Camellia said. "Or everything." She took a deep breath. "This... this is amazing." She looked around. "The whole day has been. But, Eric, why don't we ever do this at home?"

"Um, because we live in Dallas," he said. "We don't have a beach. Unless you count Lake Lewisville, but I really don't. We have concrete and skyscrapers and way too much traffic and—"

"That's not what I meant," Camellia interrupted. "I'm not talking about the beach, specifically. I mean, we never go anywhere. We don't go out in public." They hadn't since they got back from Miami. "Ever. We hang out at my house or your house. When we other plans, like to go to a restaurant, you change your mind, and promise me next time we'll go out."

And the next time was the same. They ate in, and they talked and laughed and had great sex, but lately Camellia couldn't help but wonder if there shouldn't be something more. Perhaps because her daughter had unwittingly planted that seed of doubt. "Is it because you don't want to be seen with me? Am I your dirty little secret, Eric?"

"WAIT, WHAT?" ERIC HAD been on his knees, attempting to comfort her, but when she threw that one at him, he sank completely to the ground. "Did you really just say that, because I thought I heard you right, but I'm having trouble believing it." He shook his head, still trying to clear it and make sense of the whole conversation. "You think I'm embarrassed to be seen with you? What the hell, Cami?"

"Well, aren't you?"

"No. Not even remotely close." As the initial shock wore off, anger and frustration set in. Anger that she would question him and think such a thing, and frustration because his own actions must have somehow, in some tangible way, played into those thoughts.

Eric dragged himself to his feet and then held out a hand to her. "C'mon. Get up."

She did, with minimal help, assuring Eric that she wasn't hurt, at least not physically, as she said. Good, but he was more worried about the rest.

"There's a bench over here," he said, leading her to it. "Let's sit and talk where we aren't blocking people's paths. Okay?"

After a second, Camellia nodded. "Okay, yes." She took a deep breath. "I'm sorry for the mini-meltdown."

"It's all right. Happens to everyone from time to time." Eric raked a tired hand through his hair. "Help me figure out where this is coming from, though. Please. Why would you ever think

I'm ashamed to be seen with you?" It was so far from the truth, he couldn't believe they were even having a conversation about it, yet here they were.

"Because—"

"No. Don't say it. I don't want to hear the 'F' word right now."

She smiled, at least slightly, as she wiped the last stay tear from her face. "I was going to say 'fluffy.'"

"That's better, but not by much," Eric said. "If you really think that's what I care about, what I see when I look at you, then I'm not sure you've learned anything about me during the time we've been together. Maybe that's my fault, and I need to do better."

"You're used to dating skinny, beautiful women, not ones with my emotional baggage," Camellia said.

"Oh, believe me, they can have baggage, too. As do I." Eric choked out a laugh before turning serious. "I'm going to say something here, and I want you to listen. Can you give me that courtesy before you write me off as just another asshole who's made you feel self-conscious because you don't fit some stupid societal ideal about what makes a woman attractive?"

Camellia nodded. "I'm listening."

"Good." Eric folded a leg under him, turning sideways on the bench so he could look her head on. "I've seen the picture of you from four years ago, and you're right about one thing. If our paths had crossed back then, I probably wouldn't have been interested in you," he said. "No. Check that. I know I wouldn't have been, but not because of your weight. By your own admission, you weren't a happy person back then."

"No. I was miserable," she said.

"And I couldn't have handled that, because I've been through too much myself to surround myself with negative people," he told her. "That's one of the reasons I love you. Because you're not that person, not anymore. Sure, you have occasional setbacks and flashes of self-doubt. You've overcome a lot, but you're an overwhelmingly positive person. You're smart and strong and passionate, and you've got a great sense of humor, and just like the colors you chose for your shop, you radiate happiness, and it's absolutely beautiful. You're beautiful," he said. "You need to start believing that, because I think you're fucking gorgeous, Cami. Inside and out."

"You do?"

"Yes."

"And did you say you love me?" she asked. "Because I want to be clear…"

"I did," he confirmed. "I was going to wait until tonight, on the boat, to tell you, but it kind of slipped out. It's all good, though. I meant it. I'm not taking it back."

"Boat?" Camellia blinked rapidly. "What boat, Eric?"

"Right. I guess I should tell you why we're here. I was planning to when we were walking along the beach, but then somebody had this idea that they wanted to run and just took off…"

"Let's forget about that, or at least my very ungraceful splat in the sand." Camellia waved her hands in front of her. "I want to hear about this boat thing."

"We're going out on a yacht tonight, to have drinks and dinner by the moonlight," Eric said. "Do you know Killian Moss, the pitcher from the San Antonio Riverhawks?"

"I know of him. Anna's boyfriend is a baseball player, and he's a big fan." Her eyes widened. "Is he one of your friends in high places?"

"He is, yeah." Eric grinned. "Killian hosts a special event for his charity here on South Padre Island every year. Well, this will be the third year he's done it, and I'm his emcee," he explained. "It's a good gig, because I know sports better than flowers, and Killian and his wife are great people. They also own a yacht, and tonight they've invited some of their friends on board for dinner, kind of a lead-up to the charity thing tomorrow. Some of his teammates and their significant others, people from his foundation, and there will probably be some Hollywood types, since Killian's wife is an actress."

"I know who she is. Lorna Richards. She's like a two-time Oscar winner. And now I'm going to be on a yacht with her?" Camellia shook her head. "Is this really happening?"

"Yes. The invitation includes me and a guest of my choosing," he said. "And I choose you, because I can't wait to show you off."

"You're serious? You sound serious."

"I'm serious. If you want to go, that is."

"Obviously, I'll go. I'd be an idiot not to," she said. "You must think I am an idiot."

"Not even close," Eric assured her. "If I've done anything to make you doubt, even for a second, that I am anything but proud to be with you, then I'm sorry. I think maybe I'm a little selfish and I don't want to share you with others, plus you said you have a hard time with crowds, and I didn't want you to be uncomfortable or self-conscious..." He hoped she could understand that.

"If you want to though, and if I need to convince you I'm serious, we'll go to the Cowboys game next Sunday," he said. "I'll rent out the videoboard at AT&T Stadium to tell everyone there how I feel about you."

"Eighty some thousand people? No thanks," she said. "Let's start a little smaller."

"Sure. The Stars game, then? American Airlines Center? Nineteen thousand," Eric said. "What do you think?"

"Hmm." Her brow furrowed. "That's a possibility. I do like hockey," Camellia said after a minute. "I actually have something else in mind, though."

"Name it."

"Next Wednesday, the local chamber of commerce is having a luncheon, and I'm sort of the guest of honor."

"Sort of?"

"Okay, I am." She smiled, and her whole face lit up. "I'm getting an award. Nothing special. Just the business owner of the month, but—"

"What? That's fantastic, and extremely well-deserved."

"Thanks. Anyway, I'm hoping you'll come with me to the luncheon," she said. "Anna will be there, and I could probably invite Alison, but I'd really like to have you there, Eric."

"Then I'll be there," he said without so much as a second's hesitation. "Well, on one condition, that is."

"What's that?"

"Will you introduce me to everyone as your hot and sexy boyfriend?" He grinned.

"Mmm." Camellia rubbed at her chin. "Can we just go with boyfriend?" she asked. "It's a group of civic leaders, and I'm supposed to be a respectable businesswoman and all..."

"Okay, fine. I can live with boyfriend." He leaned over and kissed her cheek. "As long as I know you think I'm hot and sexy."

"Definitely," Camellia said. "How much time do we have before we have to get ready to hob knob with your friends in high places?"

Eric looked at his watch. "A couple hours. Why? Do you want to run along the beach some more?"

"No. I thought we'd go back to the hotel, and I can work on showing you how sexy I think you are, while you show me how gorgeous you think I am."

"Ah, mutual goals. I love the way you think."

Chapter Sixteen

Eric stepped out of the shower, dried off, and wrapped the towel around his waist. Camellia had nixed the nixed the idea of showering together, insisting it would be too dangerous. He didn't know if she was more concerned about a risk of falling during whatever water sports they inevitably engaged in or that engaging in those sports would make them late for dinner. Eric was confident he could keep her from falling, but yeah... they would've been late. For sure.

Camellia was already dressed in black pants and a black and white diagonal striped shirt, and she was trying to fasten a necklace without the benefit of a mirror, and while also trying keep her hair out of the way.

"Here, let me." He stepped behind her to help fasten the necklace.

"Thanks." She let go of her hair, allowing it to fall to her shoulders.

"You look gorgeous." Eric moved closer to her, putting his hands on her hips. It was then he discovered that it wasn't pants and a shirt she wore, but rather a one-piece jumpsuit. Sexy, and he was already thinking about how best to get it her out of it later.

"Get away from me, Eric. I don't want you touching me."

"That wasn't what you were saying forty minutes ago," he reminded her with a smirk. Still, he did as she asked and backed away.

"That's the point. I can't have you getting all... amorous... and making us late," Camellia insisted. "We're supposed to be going on a yacht. With Lorna Freaking Richards. Also, it's your job."

"Amorous. That is such a beautiful word." Eric dropped the towel from his waist and retrieved a pair of boxer briefs from the drawer, noting with a satisfied smile that Camellia watched him as he did. "And I'll be on my best behavior and make sure we're on time. This is a good gig for me, and I plan to keep it." He selected a royal blue shirt from the closet. "I was merely pointing out that you are a stunningly beautiful woman." Even better, she was his, and Eric didn't plan on letting her go anytime soon.

"Thank you. Tonight, I feel beautiful." She did a little twirl. "I bought this outfit a few weeks ago when I was shopping with Anna," Camellia said. "I was hesitant to even try it on, because I was afraid it would look awful on me, but she convinced me to try it. Then when I had it on, she told me I had to buy it, because you'd love it."

"She was right." Eric finished buttoning his shirt and pulled on a pair of gray pants. "I still can't decide if your daughter likes me or not."

"I think she mostly does, on a good day," Camellia said, "but she's also a little wary."

"Then I guess have more work to do to convince her that I am worthy of her incredible mother's love and affection." He fastened his watch and pick up a comb from the dresser. "That's cool, because I like a good challenge."

Eric ran the comb through his hair. "Ready whenever you are."

"Are you serious?" Camellia looked at him incredulously. "Men. You have it so easy. Five minutes, and you're ready to go. Meanwhile, women spend hours in front of a mirror trying to impress your species, and it's still not usually good enough." She shook her head as she retreated into the bathroom, "Give me five more minutes, okay?"

It was closer to ten before she emerged, but Eric wasn't going to say anything. He also decided not to point out that she didn't look much different than when she'd gone in there, except for a little lipstick. Heck, hadn't he already told her she was gorgeous before?

"We can go now," Camellia announced, "if you can just grab my purse? It's the little black one on the table there."

"Got it." Eric grabbed the purse, as well as his phone from the nightstand, which he slipped into his pocket. "And these." He picked up her crutches.

"No. Leave those here," she said. "In fact, they shouldn't have even come on this trip."

He knew what she meant or thought he did. "You don't have to do this, Cami. There are stairs going out to the yacht, and I don't want you to lose your balance. If anybody says anything to you, or makes you feel self-conscious, I'm throwing them off the boat."

To Eric's surprise, Camellia laughed. "I'd rather you just throw the crutches off the boat, but I suppose that's not practical, either. I'll hang onto them, reluctantly, because I never know how long this remission is going to last. I am not, however, taking them on that boat."

Her voice was determined, and Eric knew better than to argue. Besides, he got tripped on one word. "Did you say remission?"

"I did." She grinned. "That was the good news I got at my check-up this morning, and why I wanted to go out to dinner at Monarch to celebrate," Camellia said. "But a yacht is better."

"We'll go to Monarch," Eric said. "I'll get reservations for Sunday as soon as we get back." He pulled her into his arms and kissed her. "I am so happy for you, Cami. I'd like to pick you up and spin you around right now."

"Please, don't. You'll throw out your back, and then we'll really be late."

"Ever the voice of pragmatism." Eric grabbed the car keys and the room key. "Fine. No spinning. Let's go mingle with my friends in high places," he said. "I can't wait for them to meet you."

CAMELLIA WAS PRETTY sure her jaw dropped when they pulled up to the dock and she saw the yacht. Not that she'd seen a lot of yachts in her life, but this looked like a nice one. "That's the boat we're going on?"

"Yep. We'll cruise around the gulf a bit, have a drink on the upper deck while we watch the moon rise," Eric said. "Then a late dinner."

"It sounds perfect. You weren't kidding about your friends." This was all rather surreal for her.

"I told you. High places." He parked the car and hurried over to the passenger side to help her out. "Have I told you lately how gorgeous you look?"

"Once or twice, but I don't get tired of hearing it." She accepted Eric's outstretched hand.

"I'll have to mingle and network a little bit," he said as they walked along the dock to the boat, "but I promise I won't leave your side for very long."

"It's okay. I'm not a delicate wallflower. I can mingle, too, and make conversation." Besides, she wanted to meet Lorna.

"I know you can. You'll probably charm everyone here," Eric said.

Before Camellia could reply, a tall and exceedingly handsome man appeared in the doorway of the yacht. "Eric! There you are. And you're not alone." His eyes widened in an expression of mock shock. "Well, I'll be darned. It's actually true." The man turned around and yelled back toward the boat, "Lor, Eric's here, and he brought a woman."

Camellia recognized his accent as Alabama, or possibly eastern Georgia, and since he appeared to be the owner of the yacht, assumed he was their baseball star host. "You must be Mr. Moss."

"Yes, but it's Killian, please," he said, extending a hand. "My pleasure."

"I'm Camellia Harris, and I'm trying to place your accent. Are you from Alabama?"

"La Grange, Georgia," he replied, naming a border town Camellia knew. "Very close, and I went to college at 'Bama. You?"

"Greenville," she answered, "and I went to Auburn."

"Ouch." He put hand to his chest. "Questionable choice in schools aside, I think I like you," Killian said, "although I have to ask what a fine and beautiful southern girl as yourself is doing with this dirtbag."

"Damn it, Killian," Eric said. "She still thinks I'm a nice guy. Can you please not ruin this for me before we've even had a drink?"

Camellia laughed, enjoying their obvious teasing banter, as they were joined by a stunning redhead whom Camellia recognized from some of her favorite movies.

"He's right. Behave, Killian. It's not like Eric's ever brought a date before." To Camellia, she said, "I'm Lorna, Killian's wife. What did you say your name was?"

"Camellia. Like the flower. It's nice to meet you. I'm a huge fan of your work, especially *Passing Through*," she said, referring to a movie that earned Lorna an Oscar a few years before.

"Thanks. It's one of my favorites as well," Lorna said. "My good friend Reece White, who directed it, will be here tonight, along with his husband. I'll introduce you."

"I'd like that." Camellia tried not to sound starstruck, but it wasn't easy. Anna would flip when she found out her mom spent the evening on a yacht with Hollywood A-listers and Major League baseball players.

"Perfect," Lorna said. "I think it's a good time for the guys to get us drinks while we talk. Come on, let me show you around the boat."

Camellia followed her, stepping onto the yacht. "It's beautiful, and I'm still having a hard time believing that I'm actually here."

Eric and Killian headed in one direction, presumably to get drinks, and Lorna led her in another. "You haven't seen anything yet. Let me take you up to the main deck."

Camellia didn't want to ask how many decks there were, so she followed Lorna up a narrow stairway, pleased at how easy it was to handle them.

"Here we go. Main deck," Lorna said. "We have a bedroom on this level, plus a sitting room and dining area. This is where dinner will be, a little later, but we'll have cocktail hour on the top deck because it's beautiful at dusk."

"That sounds amazing," Camellia said. "Thank you for having me."

"It's a pleasure. I've known Eric for three years, and this is the first time he's ever brought a woman along with him," the actress said. "How long have you been seeing each other?"

"A little more than a month," Camellia said. "We went to high school together, though."

"How fun." Lorna smiled. "When Eric called Killian earlier and said he was bringing his girlfriend along this weekend, I told my husband that this must be serious."

"Oh." Camellia wasn't sure what to say. Eric called her his girlfriend? She liked that. A lot.

"I hope that doesn't make you uncomfortable."

"No." Camellia shook her head. "It is getting pretty serious."

"I'm glad. Eric deserves a good woman."

"Yes, I do, and now that I've finally found one, can you please not scare her away, Lorna?"

At the sound of Eric's voice, they both turned around. "How long have you been standing there?" Camellia asked.

"Not very long." He held out a glass of wine. "Chardonnay for my beautiful girl."

She took it from him. "Thanks."

"I should probably leave you two alone and go play hostess some more," Lorna said, "but I'll find you when Reece and Courtland get here so you can meet them, Camellia."

"Great. I look forward to it."

"Me, too," Lorna said. To Eric, she added. "You're right. You've got a good one here. Try not to screw it up."

"Yes, Lorna." When she'd left them alone, Eric rolled his eyes. "That's the second time today I've received a similar warning."

"What do you mean?" Camellia frowned.

"Your daughter, this morning," Eric said. "Right before you got to the shop, she told me I better not turn out to be a douche canoe. I'm honestly not sure what that even means, but I don't think it's good."

"Oh, Lord." Camellia sighed. "It's Anna's new favorite word, and you're right, it's not good," she said. "I'm sorry. I'll have a talk with her when we get home."

"It's fine. I know she means well," Eric said. "Why don't we go up to the top deck? The view is the best from there."

"Okay." More stairs, but these weren't a problem, either. She could do this.

Camellia gasped when they emerged onto the upper deck, and she took in view of the Gulf of Mexico. Eric hadn't been kidding. The water and the skyline appeared to stretch on forever. "Wow," she said. "This is incredible. Thank you for bringing me along."

"You're welcome." Eric put an arm around her waist as they stood at the railing. "I wish I could give this to you more than once a year when I do this gig," he said, "but I can't. I'm not rich. I've got a modest house in Lewisville, a cool dog, and a five-year-old Infiniti that I'm still making payments on. I'll never be able to give you a yacht, Cami, even if you deserve one."

"Oh, Eric. I don't want a yacht. I just want a man who can make me laugh, doesn't harp on me to lose more weight and won't ever cheat on me," she said. "Oh, and who occasionally sends me flowers, even though I own a flower shop."

"Is that all? Because I'm cautiously optimistic I might be in the running here."

"You are. At least, I hope. I'm really hoping I've finally found that guy, Eric"

"You have. I can be that guy. I promise," he said, and she believed him. "I love you, Cami."

"Good. Because I love you, too."

They stood in silence for a few minutes, and then Camellia said. "One more thing, though."

"What's that?"

"I still want to go to Monarch."

Eric laughed. "I figured that was coming, and I've already made the reservation. Sunday night. The special treatment, surprise multi-course dinner, all of it. Because if anyone's worth it, you are."

Epilogue

Eric unloaded the suitcases from the rental car while Camellia handed the valet the keys and took the valet ticket number.

"Check in is right inside the revolving door there," the attendant told her.

"I know. We were here a year ago," she said.

"Then you must've enjoyed your stay. It's good to see you back."

"Thank you. And yes, we had a great time." She reached down to grab the handle of her small suitcase and wheeled it toward the entrance.

"Are you sure don't need help with that?" Eric asked.

"I'm sure. You've got your hands full with all the others." She still hadn't mastered the art of packing light, especially since this year, she was also packing for a two-week stay in Barbados once the conference was over.

"Looks like this place is as chaotic as last year," Eric observed.

"I know, but I always try to stay the event hotel when I travel for conferences," Camellia said. "And besides, the memories."

She left Eric with the bags and approached the counter. "Checking in. The last name is Harris. Wait. I mean Grady," she said. "It's Grady." Camellia really hoped the hotel clerk didn't have Anna's imagination, or she might assume that Camellia was a fugitive from justice and traveling under a fake name rather than the much more benign explanation of still getting used to her married name. She passed the clerk her driver's license. Thankfully, she'd made a visit to the DMV to update it before the trip.

Her business credit card was still under Harris, but the clerk didn't appear to be overly concerned with that. "Okay. You're all set, Ms. Grady. We've got you in room 814. I believe you specifically requested that when you made the reservation."

"I did, yes," she said. "Thanks for honoring that."

"You're welcome." The clerk handed her the packet with the room keys. "Your conference rate includes breakfast Saturday morning. The coupons are in here."

Camellia took the key cards and rejoined Eric. "We're all set, and I got us our special room," she told him, and he laughed.

"I love your sentimental side, Mrs. Grady."

"Mrs. Grady. I'm rather liking the way that sounds." Camellia pushed the button for the elevator.

"I hope so," her husband said. "Because you're stuck with it now, along with me, for a long time."

The elevator car opened, and a woman stepped off. "Oh my gosh, Camellia. What a coincidence. I was just wondering of you'd made it yet."

"Hi, Angie. We just got here," Camellia said. "You remember Eric, right?"

"I do, yes," Angie said. "I hope you're hosting again?"

"I am. I wouldn't miss this one."

Angie looked from him to Camellia, and then to the three suitcases Eric was trying to maneuver into the elevator and said, "Something tells me that this year, you didn't just run into each in the parking lot."

"Nope," Camellia said with a laugh. "This time we're on our honeymoon."

"What?" Angie's jaw dropped. "Okay, I admit I wondered if something was going on last year, but wow..."

"Yeah. What can I say? This conference has been very good to us."

"That's fantastic," Angie said. "I was just going to the bar to grab a drink. I hope you'll join me? I want to hear all about this."

"I'd love that," Camellia said. "Let us get our bags to the room, and I'll be down." She hoped Eric would come along, too. She wanted him to get to know Angie.

"You go, Cam," Eric said. "I'll take the bags and join you two in a few minutes."

"You sure?"

"I am." He bent down and kissed her forehead. "Five minutes. Ten, tops." He stepped on to the elevator and the doors closed.

"I guess we're going to the bar," Camellia said. The same bar where she and Eric had first connected the year before, over crab cakes and Chardonnay.

"Yay!" Angie grabbed her arm and led her that way. "I still can't believe this. You're married? To our sexy host from last year?"

"I am, yeah." There were days when Camellia didn't quite believe it, either. "It's been a heck of a year."

The proposal had come quickly, over champagne and an elaborate dinner at Monarch the night they returned from South Padre Island, and its fast timing garnered a few skeptical remarks from Anna, but Camellia brushed them aside. When something was right, it was right, and nothing had ever felt more right than being with Eric.

Besides, the fast proposal turned into a long engagement, as they endeavored to negotiate timing, jobs, houses, and pets. In the end, they'd settled on her house, because it didn't have stairs, it was close to her shop and closer to the airport than Eric's, which made it convenient for him. It meant an adjustment for Lizzie, and a few changes to the backyard, but now Eric's dog had settled in nicely, and Camellia still had her garden, albeit a slightly smaller one.

Marriage at this stage of their lives, especially since neither of them had ever done it before, meant compromise. It was worth it, though, because she'd never been happier.

"Did you just get married then?" Angie said when they had their drinks and were seated at a table. "Since this is your honeymoon?"

"A few weeks ago," Camellia said. "We timed the wedding for after my busy season, with the honeymoon to follow this conference, since it's kind of special for us."

"I'll say. Well, you look fantastic," Angie said. "Marriage obviously agrees with you."

"Thanks. I think so, too." She'd experienced one MS flare-up, which Camellia blamed on stress and pushing herself too much around the time of Anna's college graduation, but thankfully it had been short, and she was back to feeling good.

"I even got down to my goal weight in time for my daughter's graduation," she said. "Granted, it only lasted a few weeks, but that's okay. It'll happen again. Besides, my husband loves me the way I am." Being confident in that was a wonderful feeling, but not as nice as when his arms came around her from behind her chair.

"That's right. He does."

Camellia herself blush as she turned her head to look up at him. "How long have you been standing there?"

"Not long," he said. "I see you two have drinks already, but I think we need a bottle of champagne. What do you say, Angie?"

"I won't turn it down," she said. "This is my vacation, and I'd love to celebrate with you."

"Then champagne it is," Eric said. "I'm on my honeymoon, and besides it took me forty-five years to find the woman I wanted to spend the rest of my life with. If anything calls for expensive champagne, that does."

Author's Note

AS ALWAYS, THANK YOU for reading. I write because I have stories in my head that are demanding to be told and because it's cheaper than therapy, but it is always gratifying to know there are readers who enjoy my stories. I hope you enjoyed Cami and Eric's.

When I began writing the Shop series books, I never quite envisioned so many spinoffs, but as soon as I wandered into the Westfield High Class of 1995 twenty-fifth reunion (in Mix Tapes & Candy Cigarettes), I knew there was a story for Camellia. I didn't immediately know what that story was, though, or rather who would be the one to bring her a happily ever after. The more I thought about it, though, I decided who better than her teenage crush and Westfield's golden boy?

I had more fun with this book than any I've written in a long time. I loved telling Cami and Eric's story and checking in with other Westfield grads again, like Alison (best supporting actress for sure) and Gina. Will there be more? Stay tuned.

Thank you to my good friend Tiffany Carby, who is the brainchild behind the various shops in the Shop series, and her designer alter-ego for the fabulous cover.

Also by Michele Shriver

Women's Fiction:
After Ten
Tears and Laughter
Aggravated Circumstances
Contemporary Romance:
Finding Forever (Reel Love series #1)
Leap of Faith
Stay with Me
Starting Over
Love & Light
Dissonance
Fade into Love (Reel Love series #2)
In Soft Focus (Reel Love series #3)
All Roads Lead to Home
Westmore Estates trilogy:
Planting a Dream
Love in Harvest
Perfect Balance (coming soon)
In the Zone series:
Strike Zone
Danger Zone
Red Zone
Attack Zone (June 2022)
The Men of the Ice Novellas:
Playing for Keeps
Crossing the Line
Winning it All
Scoring at Love
Chasing the Prize
Making an Impact
Breaking the Ice
Going all In
Beating the Odds

About the Author

Michele Shriver writes women's fiction and contemporary romance. Her books feature flawed-but-likeable characters in real-life settings. She's not afraid to break the rules, but never stops believing in happily ever after. Michele counts among her favorite things a good glass of wine, a hockey game, and a sweet and sexy book boyfriend, not necessarily in that order.

Contact:
Website: www.micheleshriver.com
Twitter: www.twitter.com/micheleshriver
Facebook: www.facebook.com/AuthorMicheleShriver
Email: micheleshriver@gmail.com
Newsletter: http://eepurl.com/323sj
For contests, special gifts, advance reader copies of my books and the chance to hang out and chat and keep up to date on all my publishing news, please consider joining my Facebook group, Michele's Mavens:
https://www.facebook.com/groups/721292531291721/

9 798201 005085